NINJA KITTIES™

NEVER GIVE UP!

Save the Castle

NINJA KITTIES™

NEVER GIVE UP!

Save the Castle

Created and illustrated by
KAYOMI HARAI

Story by
ROB HUDNUT

Happy Fox
BOOKS

Kayomi Harai – Creator and Illustrator

Born in Osaka, Japan, Kayomi Harai is a self-taught artist who began drawing and painting at an early age. Her paintings are full of imaginati and feature a wide range of animals, including cats, tigers, leopards, wolves, eagles, and dragons. She likes to use watercolors, colored pencils and pastels in her artwork and creates art digitally also. Her works have been exhibited and licensed around the world. She currently lives in Sar Jose, California.

Kayomi created Ninja Kitties as a way to remind children that they can b anything they want to be and that they should always believe in themse

Kayomi was inspired by her three mischievous kitty assistants, who she adopted from a local animal shelter. The oldest is Kitty (a tortoiseshell tabby) and the babies are Lala and Poppy (calico sisters). They have been her inspiration and joy ever since the day she brought them home.

Rob Hudnut – Author

Rob Hudnut is an award-winning writer and storyteller in children's entertainment and the owner and founder of Rob Hudnut Productions, wh he specializes in creating play- and faith-based franchises for kids. Some of their global clients include NBCUniversal, Alpha Toys, ICON Creative Studio, Kavaleer Productions, and more. Prior to starting his own producti company, Rob was the executive producer and vice president of Mattel's entertainment division for 19 years, where his work included award-winning entertainment Barbie, Hot Wheels, Fisher-Price Little People, Rescue Heroes, DC Superhero Girls, Masters of Universe, and other Mattel brands. An Emmy-nominated songwriter, Rob also co-wrote the Barbie movie, *Barbie in The Nutcracker*, and more than 50 songs for the Barbie movies, as we songs for Hot Wheels and Fisher-Price.

NINJA KITTIES and related design marks are trademarks of New Design Originals and Kayomi Harai.

Ninja Kitties Never Give Up!
Copyright © 2023 by Kayomi Harai and Happy Fox Books, an imprint of Fox Chapel Publishing Company, Inc. All rights reserved.

Reproduction of the contents is strictly prohibited without written permission from the rights holder.

Series Editor: Elizabeth Martins

ISBN 978-1-64124-303-2

Library of Congress Control Number: 2023938981

To learn more about the other great books from Fox Chapel Publishing, or to find a retailer near you, call toll-free 800-45 or visit us at *www.FoxChapelPublishing.com*.

We are always looking for talented authors. To submit an idea, send a brief inquiry to acquisitions@foxchapelpublishing.com.

Fox Chapel Publishing makes every effort to use environme friendly paper for printing.

Printed in the United States of America
First printing

Additional image credits: pages 2, and back jacket, top, yell burst: starlineart, Freepik.com; page 17, frame around art: Gi Shutterstock.com.

HI, I'M PEPPER THE WOODPECKER!

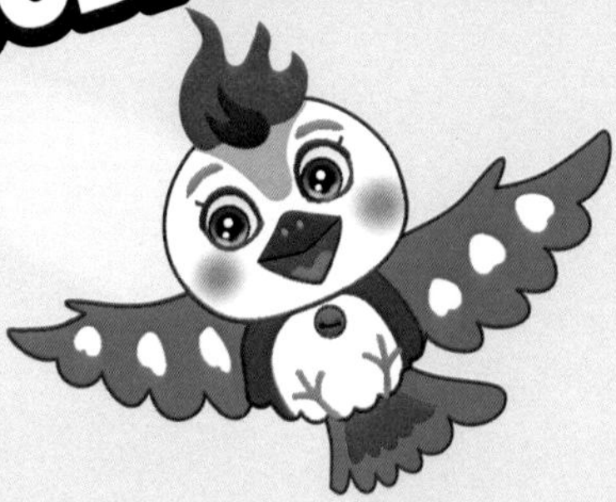

I'm the royal messenger in a place called Kitlandia. This beautiful kingdom is ruled by King Reo, Queen Mira, and their children, the royal kitties. It's also home of the Ninja Kitties who spread **NINJA GOODNESS**—kindness, confidence, love, empathy, individuality, and persistence—and keep the kingdom safe from the Fang Gang! Only the king and queen, Grandma Tabby, and I know that the Ninja Kitties are really the royal kitties!

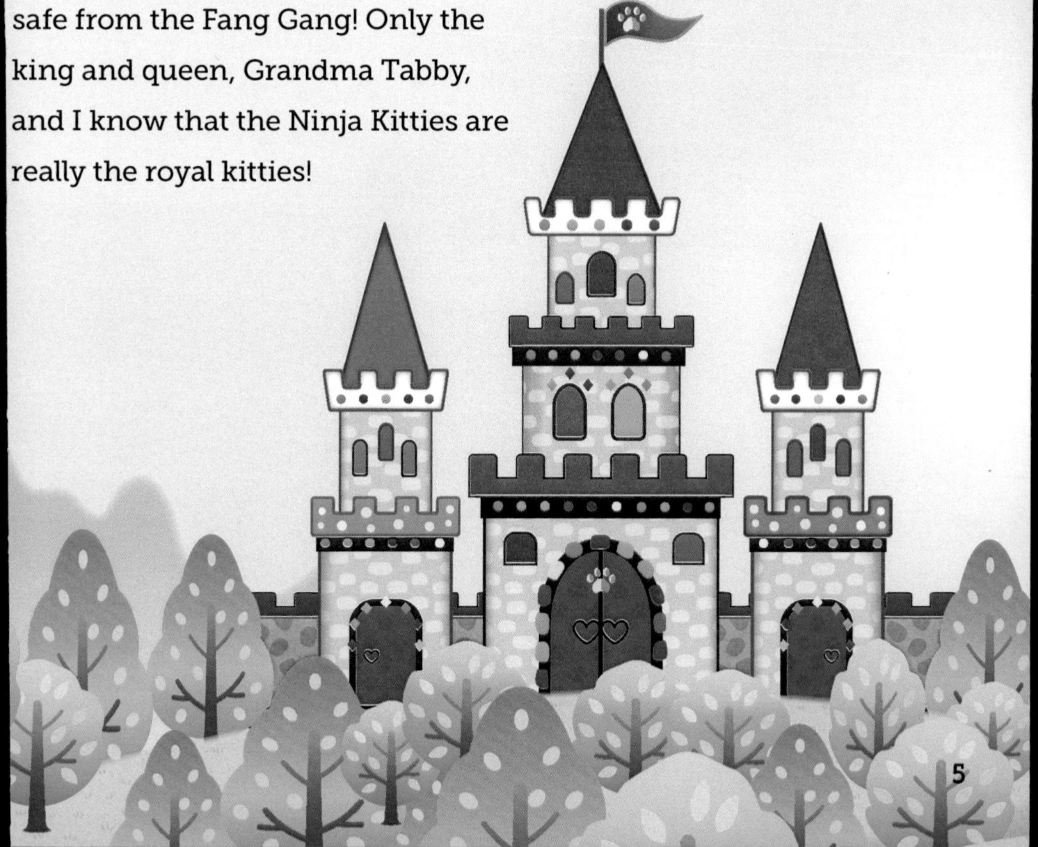

Zumi

SUPER LEAPER!

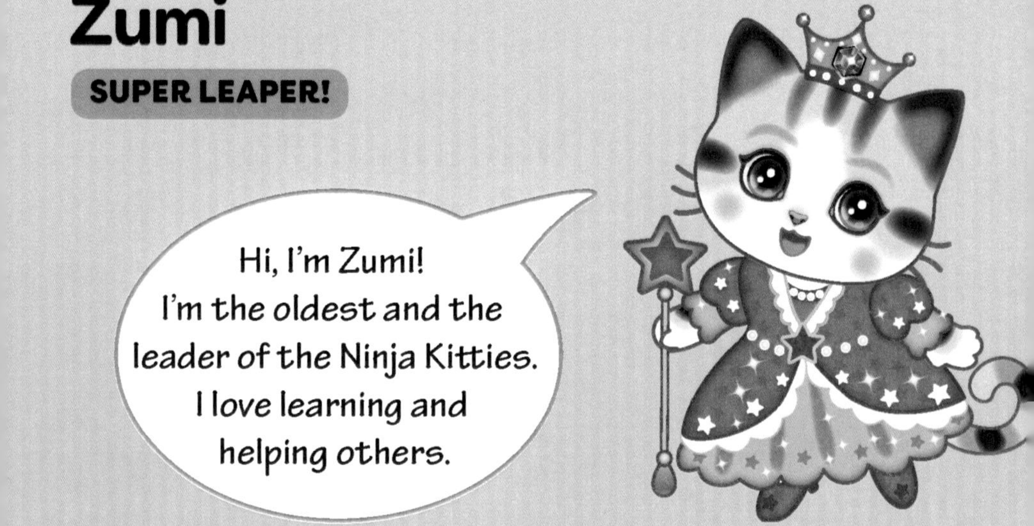

Hi, I'm Zumi!
I'm the oldest and the leader of the Ninja Kitties. I love learning and helping others.

With my super leaping skills, I can jump really high! My favorite color is pink, and my sta gem helps me leap even higher and farther.

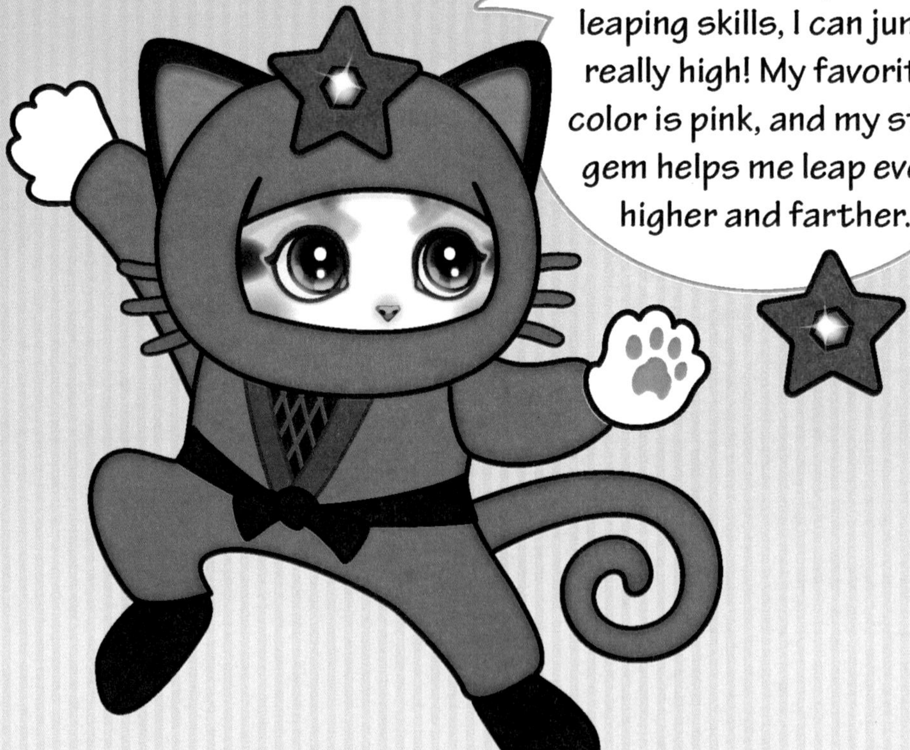

Bee-Bee

SUPER STICKY POWERS!

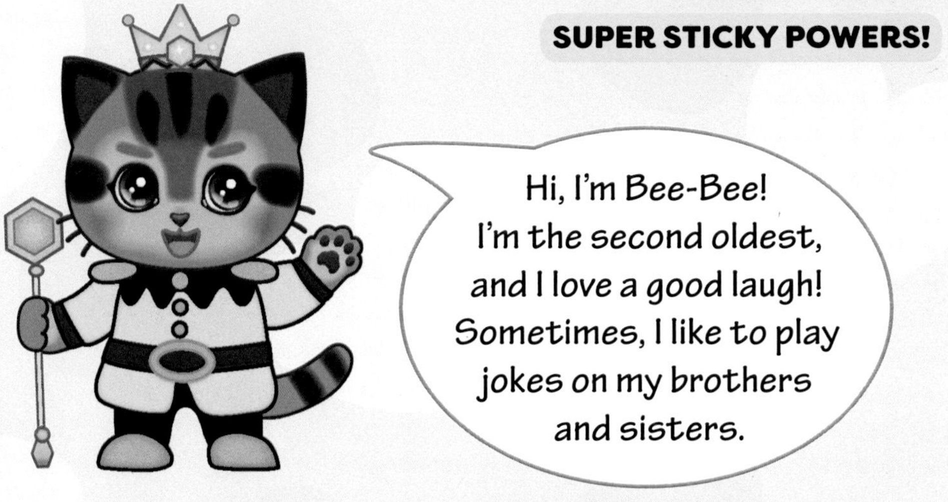

Hi, I'm Bee-Bee!
I'm the second oldest,
and I love a good laugh!
Sometimes, I like to play
jokes on my brothers
and sisters.

With my super
honey skills, I can fix
things and slow down the Fang
Gang. My favorite color is yellow,
and my gem is shaped like a
honeycomb.

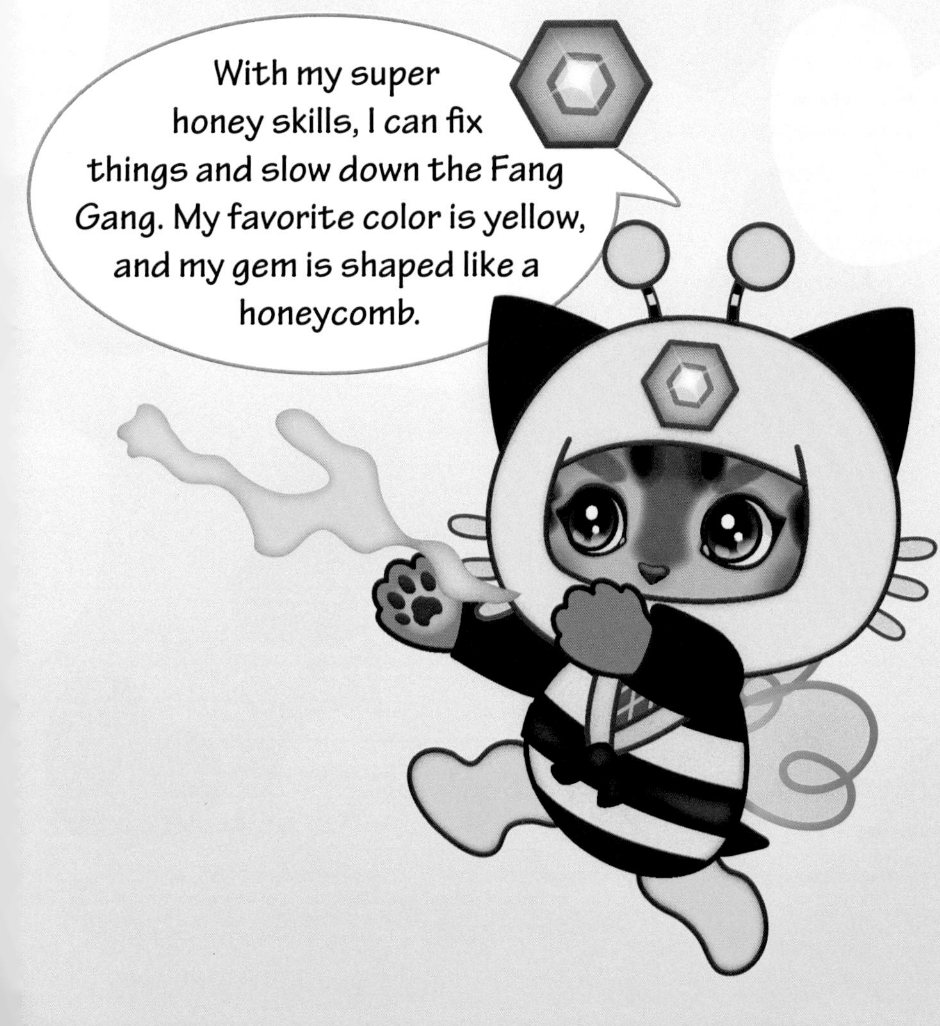

Drago

SUPER HEAT & GLOW!

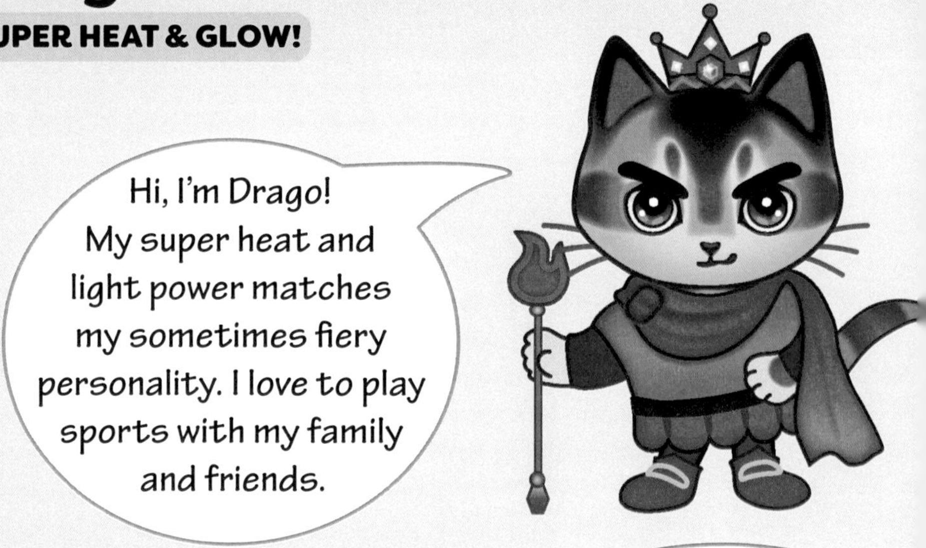
Hi, I'm Drago! My super heat and light power matches my sometimes fiery personality. I love to play sports with my family and friends.

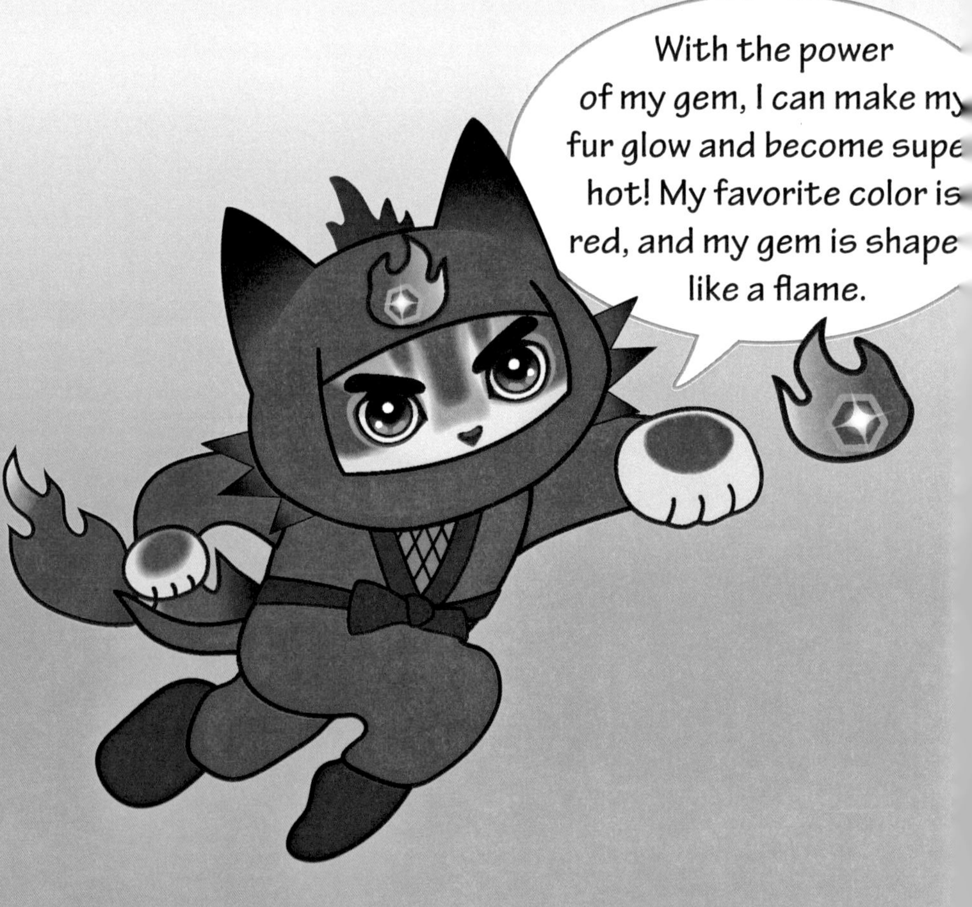
With the power
of my gem, I can make m
fur glow and become supe
hot! My favorite color is
red, and my gem is shape
like a flame.

Sora

SUPER FLYER!

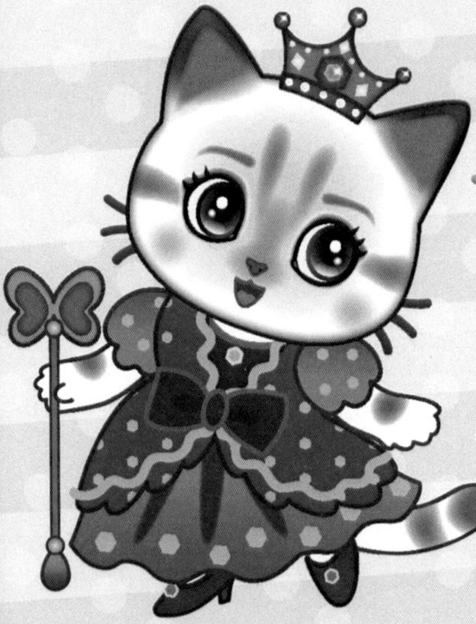

Hi, I'm Sora! My favorite color is purple, and I love to dress up.

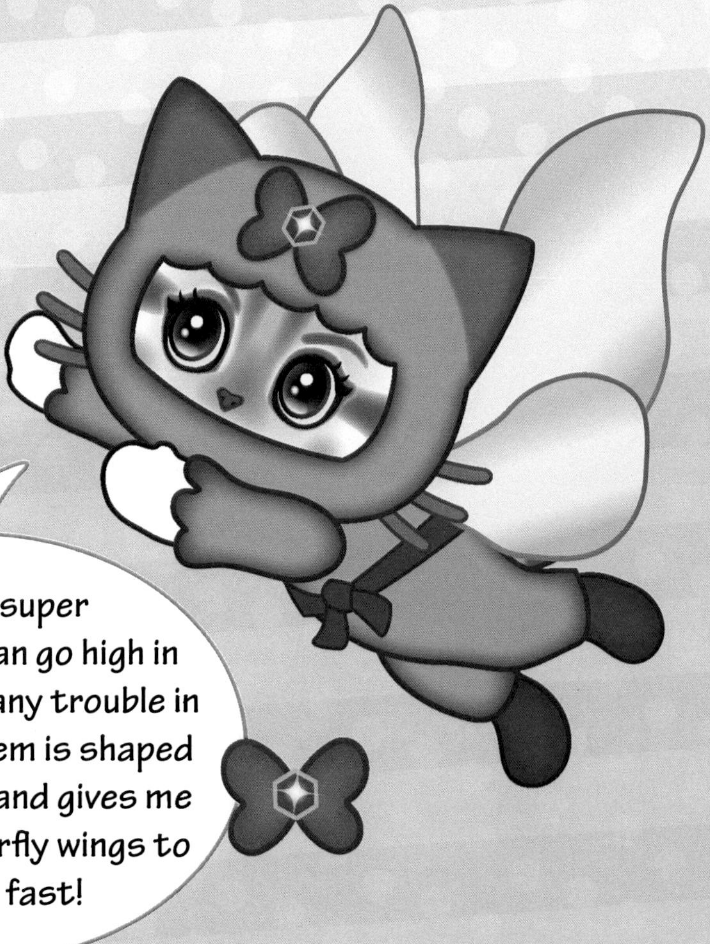

With my super flying skills, I can go high in the air and see any trouble in Kitlandia. My gem is shaped like a butterfly and gives me beautiful butterfly wings to fly really fast!

Mia

SUPER WATER POWERS!

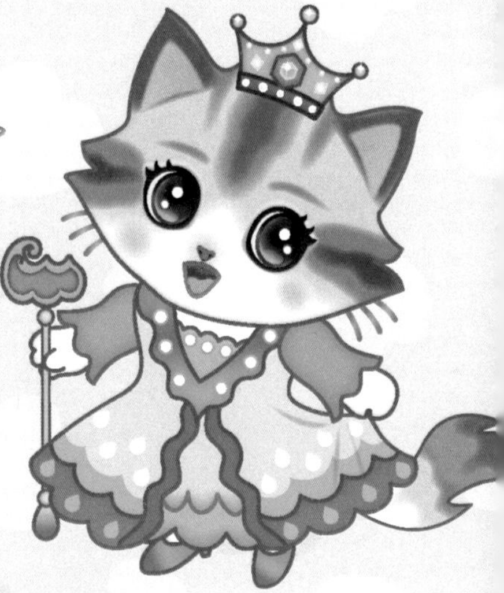
Hi, I'm Mia!
I love to swim, and I
love any type of
water sport.

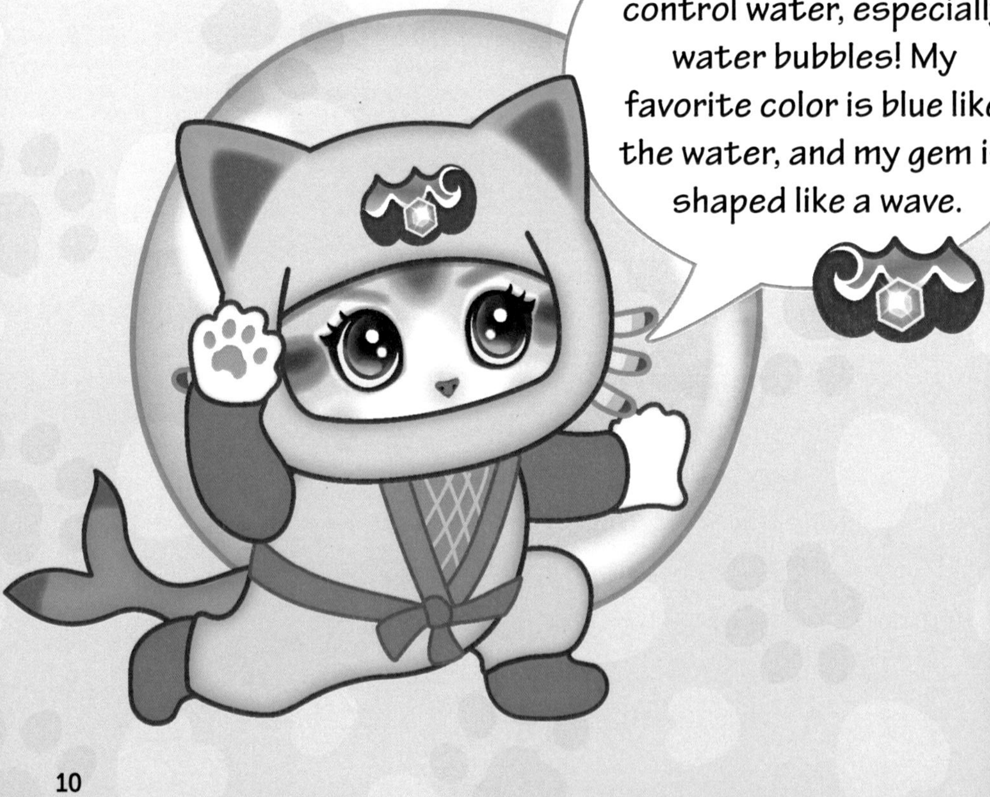
My ninja skills let me
control water, especially
water bubbles! My
favorite color is blue like
the water, and my gem is
shaped like a wave.

Leon

SUPER STRONG!

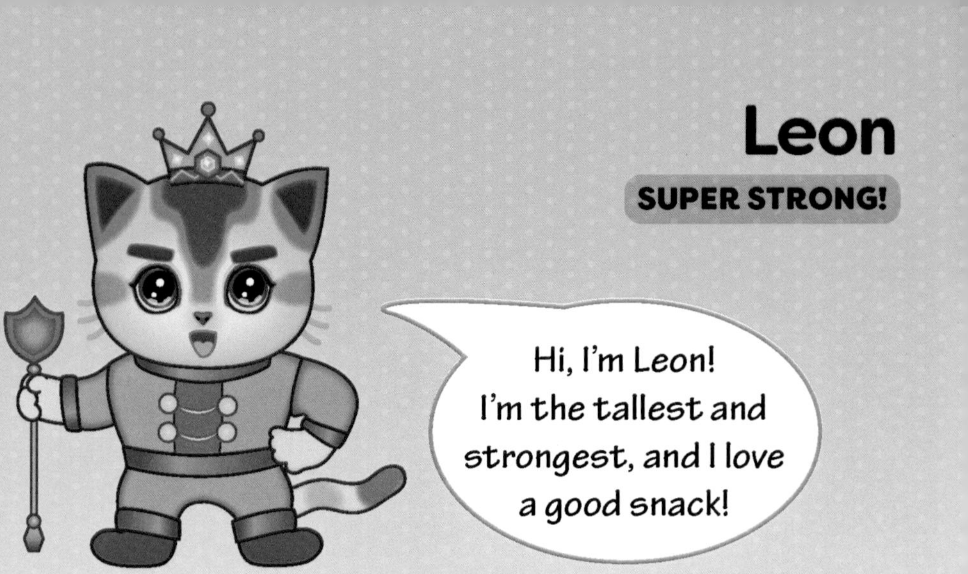
Hi, I'm Leon!
I'm the tallest and
strongest, and I love
a good snack!

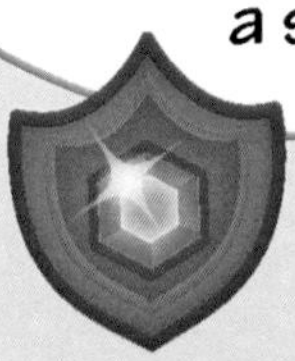
My super strength
lets me pick up or move really
heavy objects. My favorite
color is orange, and my
ninja gem is shaped like
a shield.

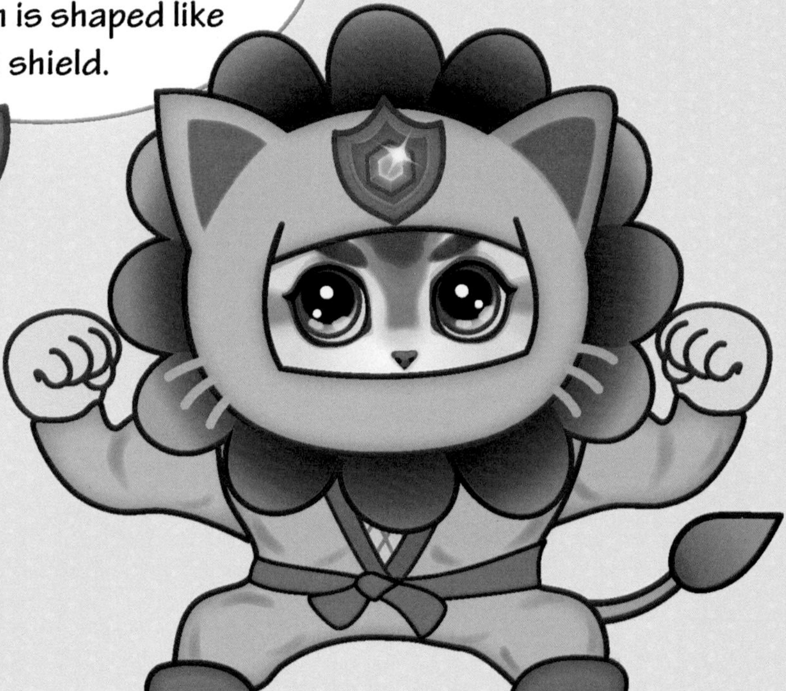

Hana

SUPER FLORAL POWERS!

Hi, I'm Hana!
I'm the youngest and
sometimes the quietest.
I like to figure things out
and come up with lots
of ideas!

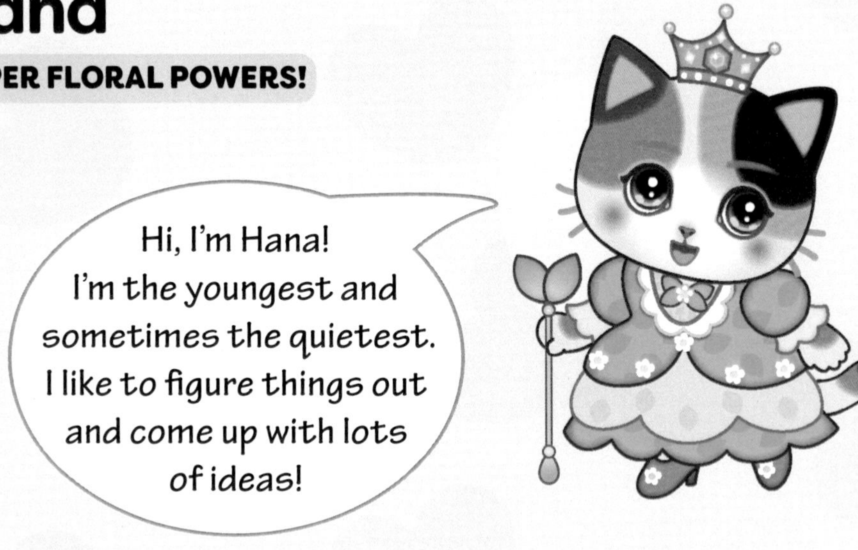

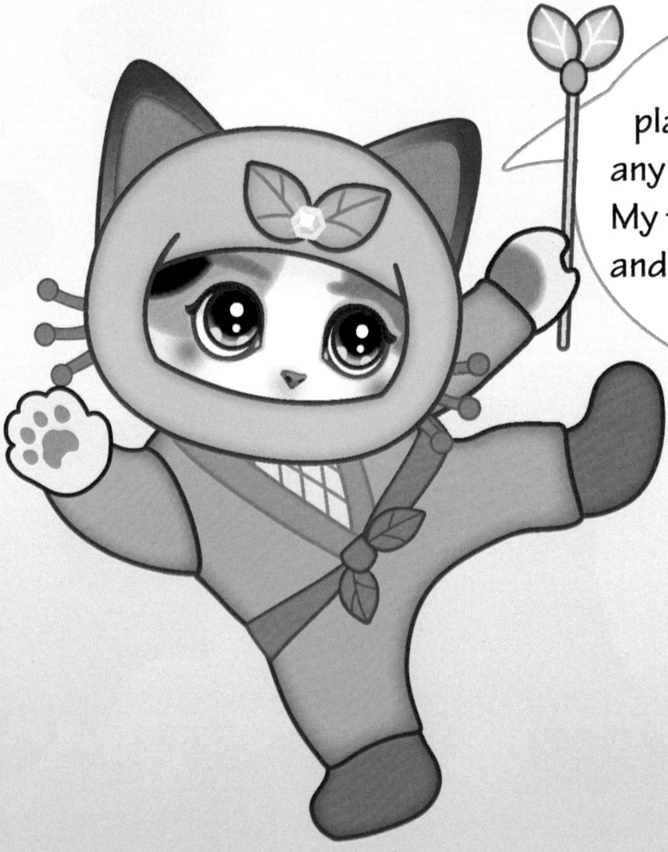

With my super
plant power, I can grow
any kind of plant or flowe
My favorite color is gree
and my gem is shaped lik
two leaves.

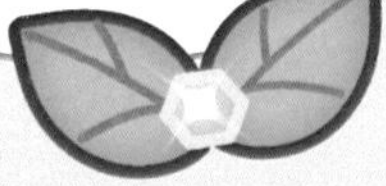

Queen Mira and King Reo

Hi, I'm Queen Mira. I'm the mother of seven royal kitties. King Reo and I teach the royal kitties to always help others, to always be respectful and kind, and to always believe in your inner strength. Along with Grandma Tabby, we are also keepers of the greatest secret in Kitlandia—the true identity of the Ninja Kitties!

Hi, I'm King Reo. Queen Mira and I watch over Kitlandia and make sure all who live here are kept safe. I sit on a great throne with wheels that helps me get around everywhere in Kitlandia. Although I can't walk like the royal kitties and Queen Mira, I can still go anywhere and focus on being the best ruler I can be.

Grandma Tabby

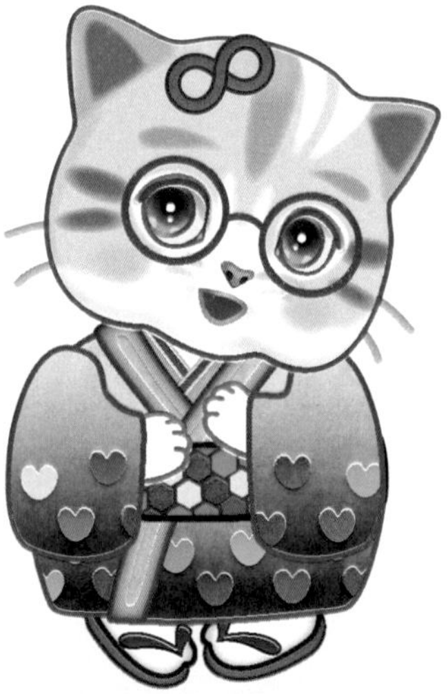

Hi, I'm Grandma Tabby, the Ninja Kitties' grandmother and trainer. I love to share a good book and a cup of tea with my grandchildren as much as I love to train with them!

I am the keeper of the Ninja Kitties' gems, and I have given one to eac of my grandchildren to boost their ninja powers. I'm happy to pass down everything I learned from being a Ninja Kitty!

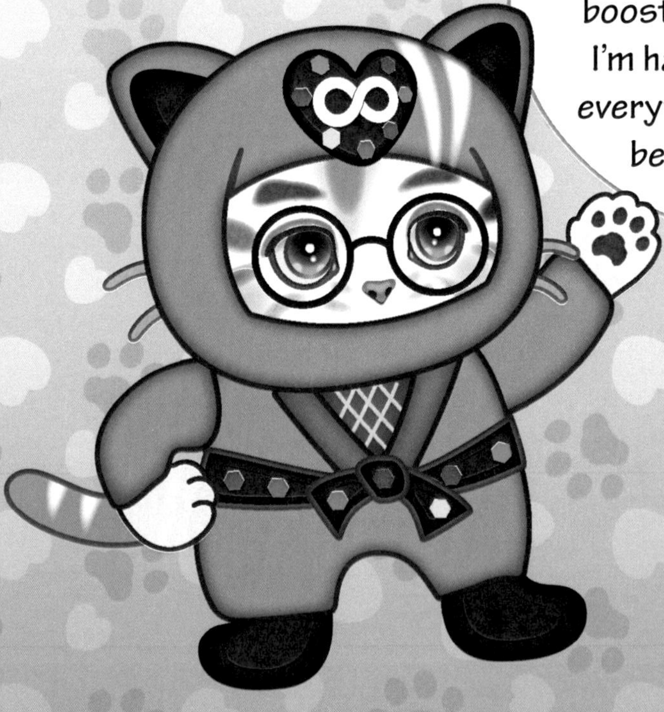

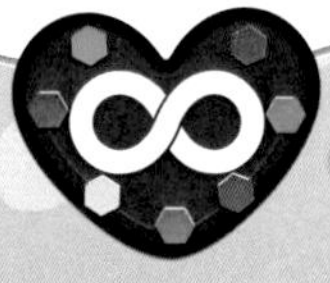

Fang Gang

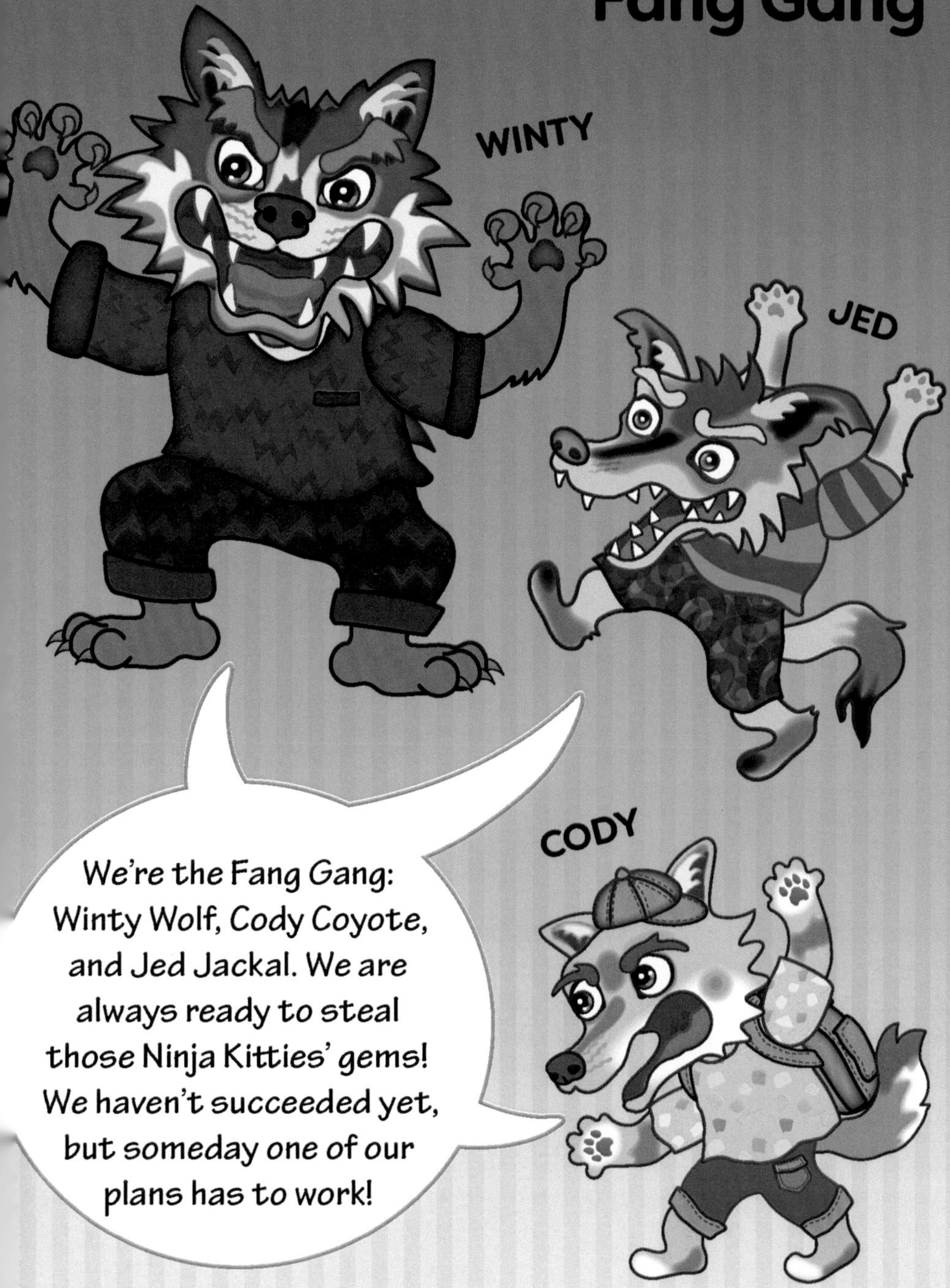
WINTY
JED
CODY
We're the Fang Gang: Winty Wolf, Cody Coyote, and Jed Jackal. We are always ready to steal those Ninja Kitties' gems! We haven't succeeded yet, but someday one of our plans has to work!

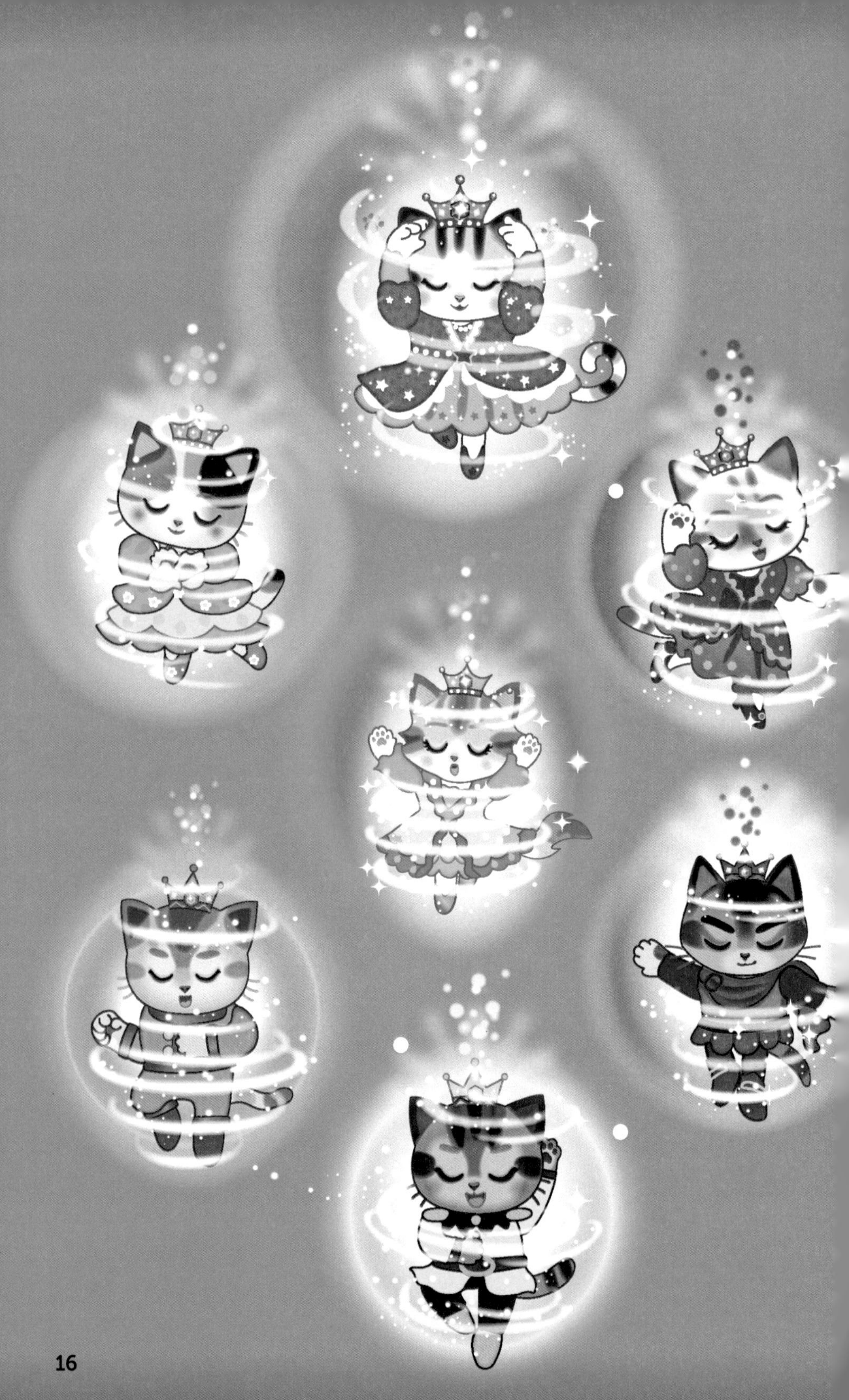

NEVER GIVE UP!

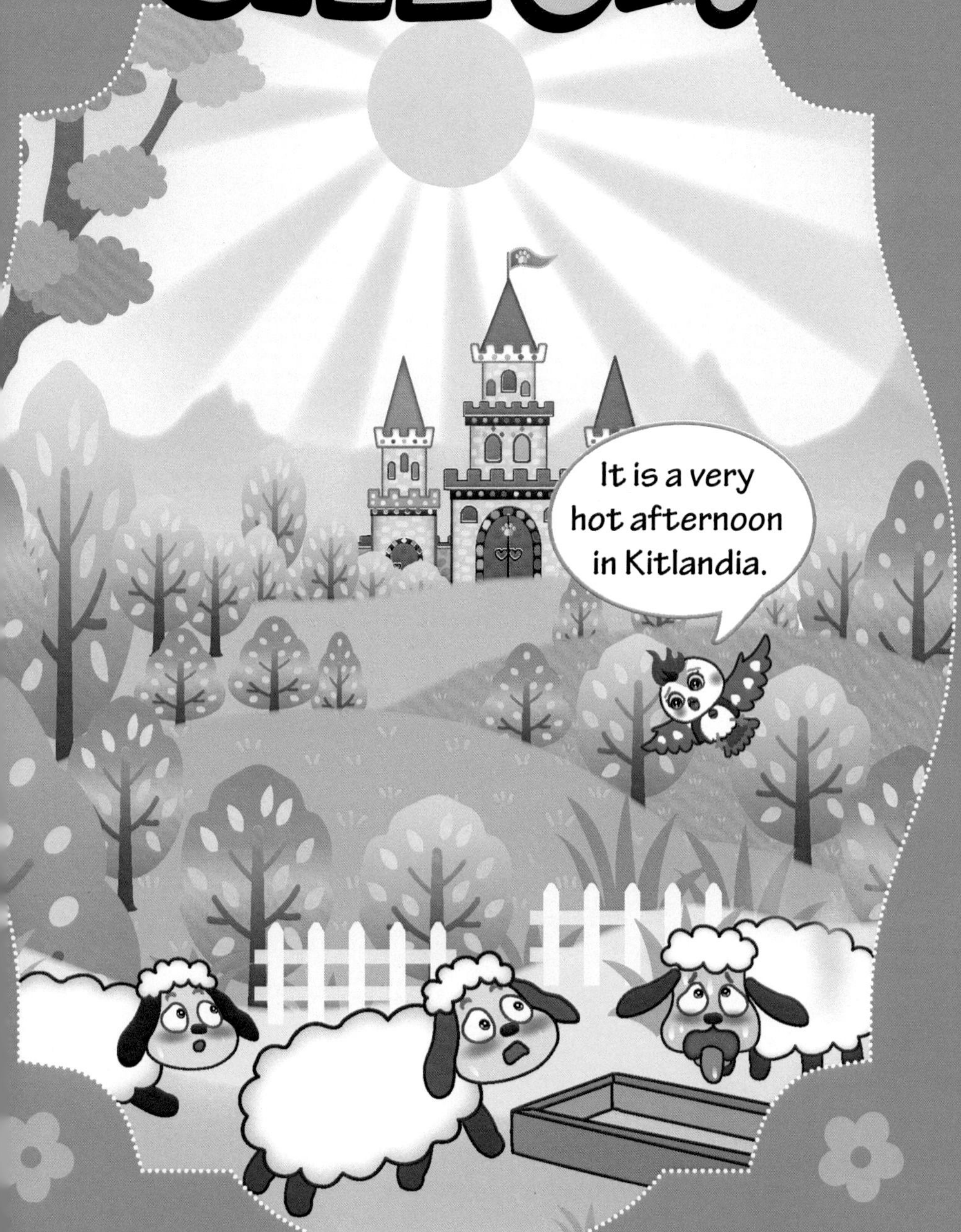
It is a very hot afternoon in Kitlandia.

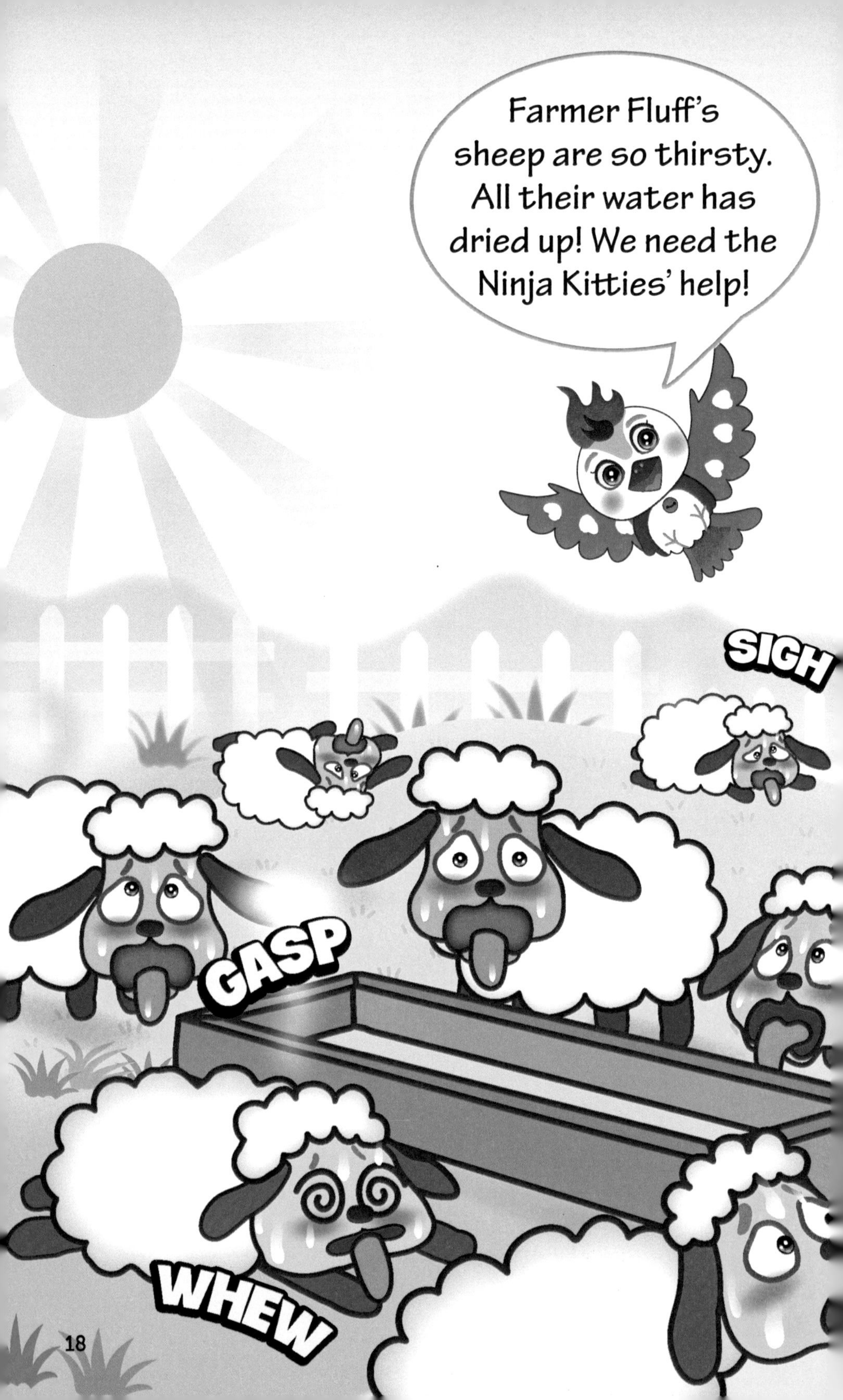
Farmer Fluff's sheep are so thirsty. All their water has dried up! We need the Ninja Kitties' help!
SIGH
GASP
WHEW

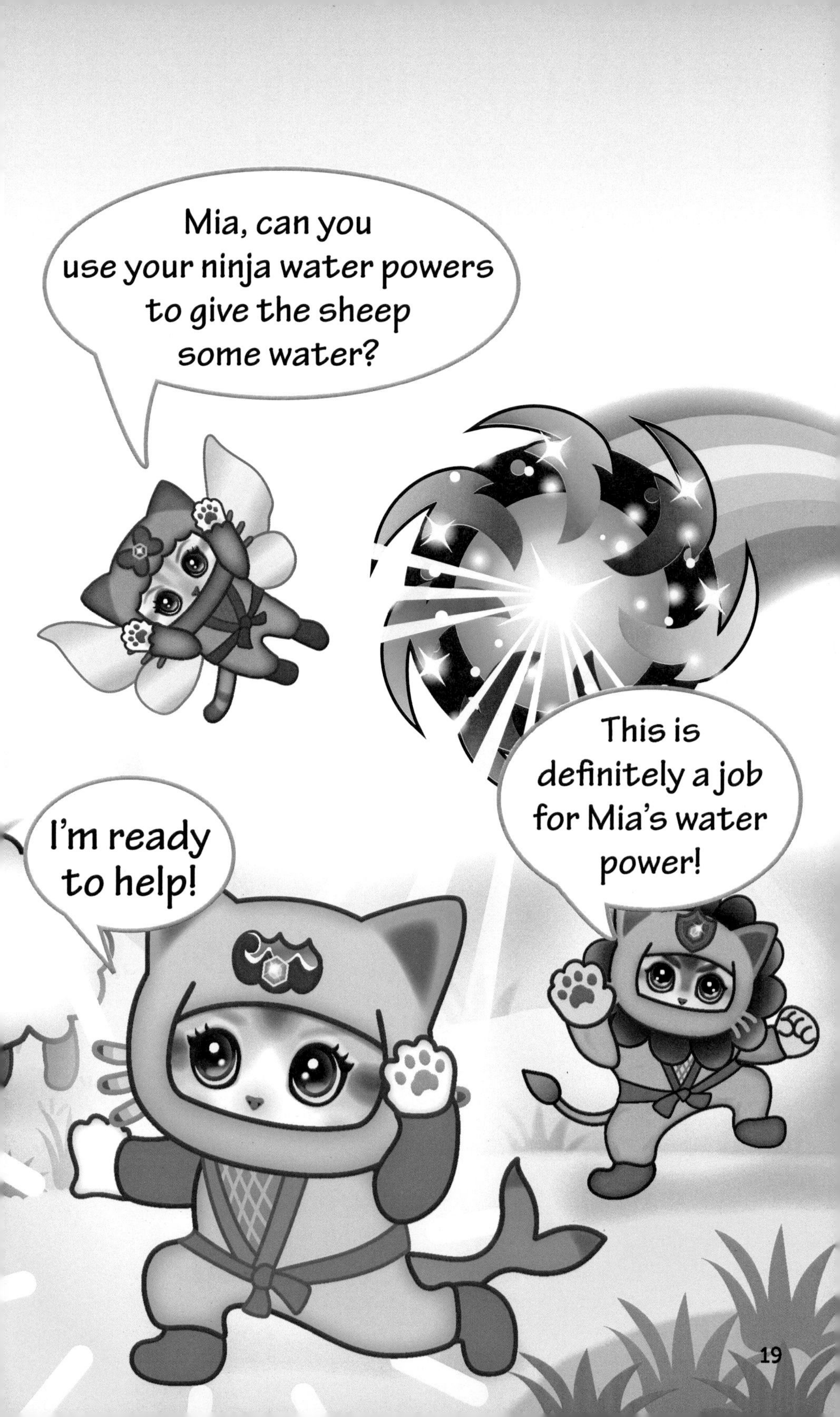
Mia, can you use your ninja water powers to give the sheep some water?
This is definitely a job for Mia's water power!
I'm ready to help!

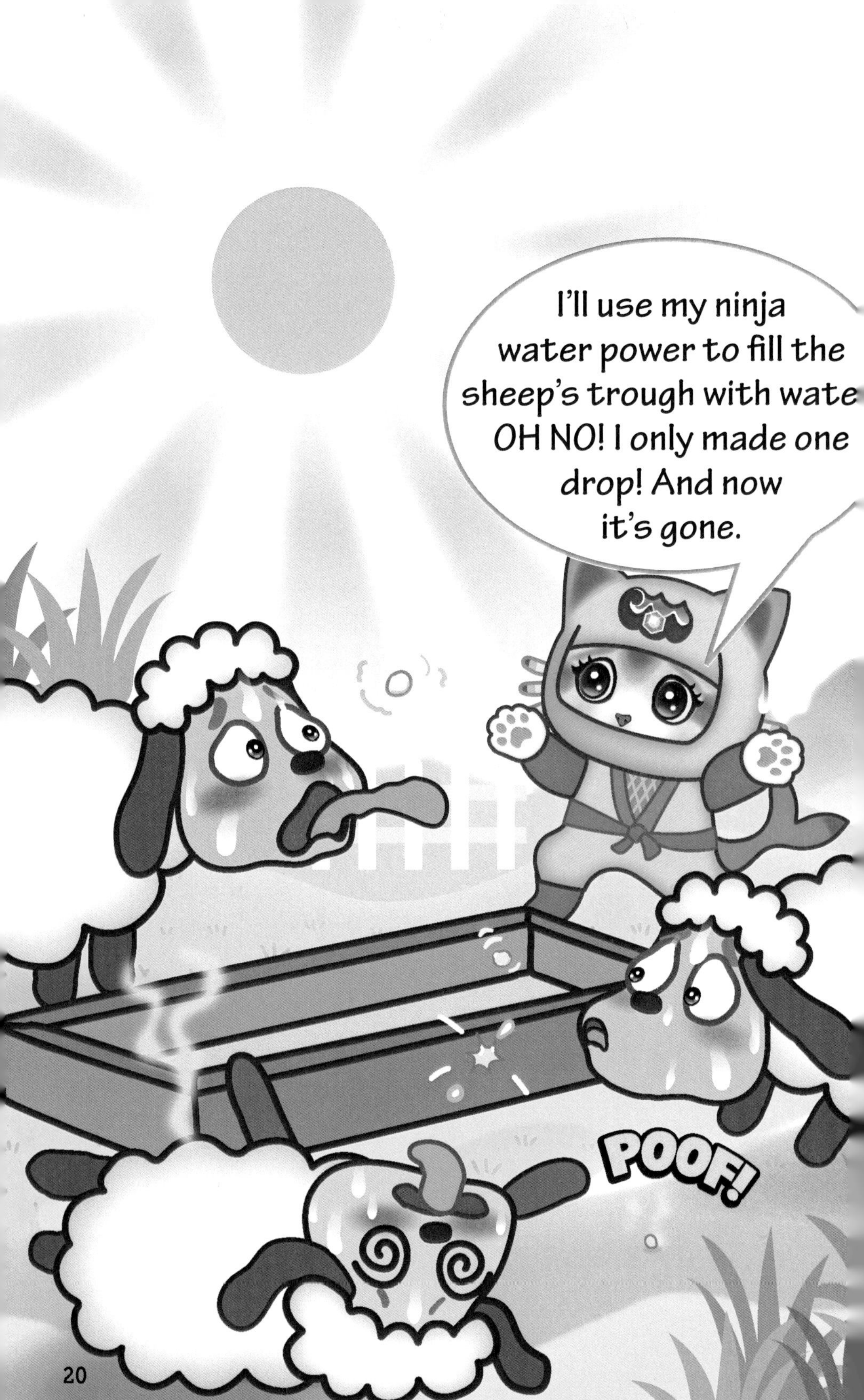
I'll use my ninja water power to fill the sheep's trough with wate OH NO! I only made one drop! And now it's gone.
POOF!

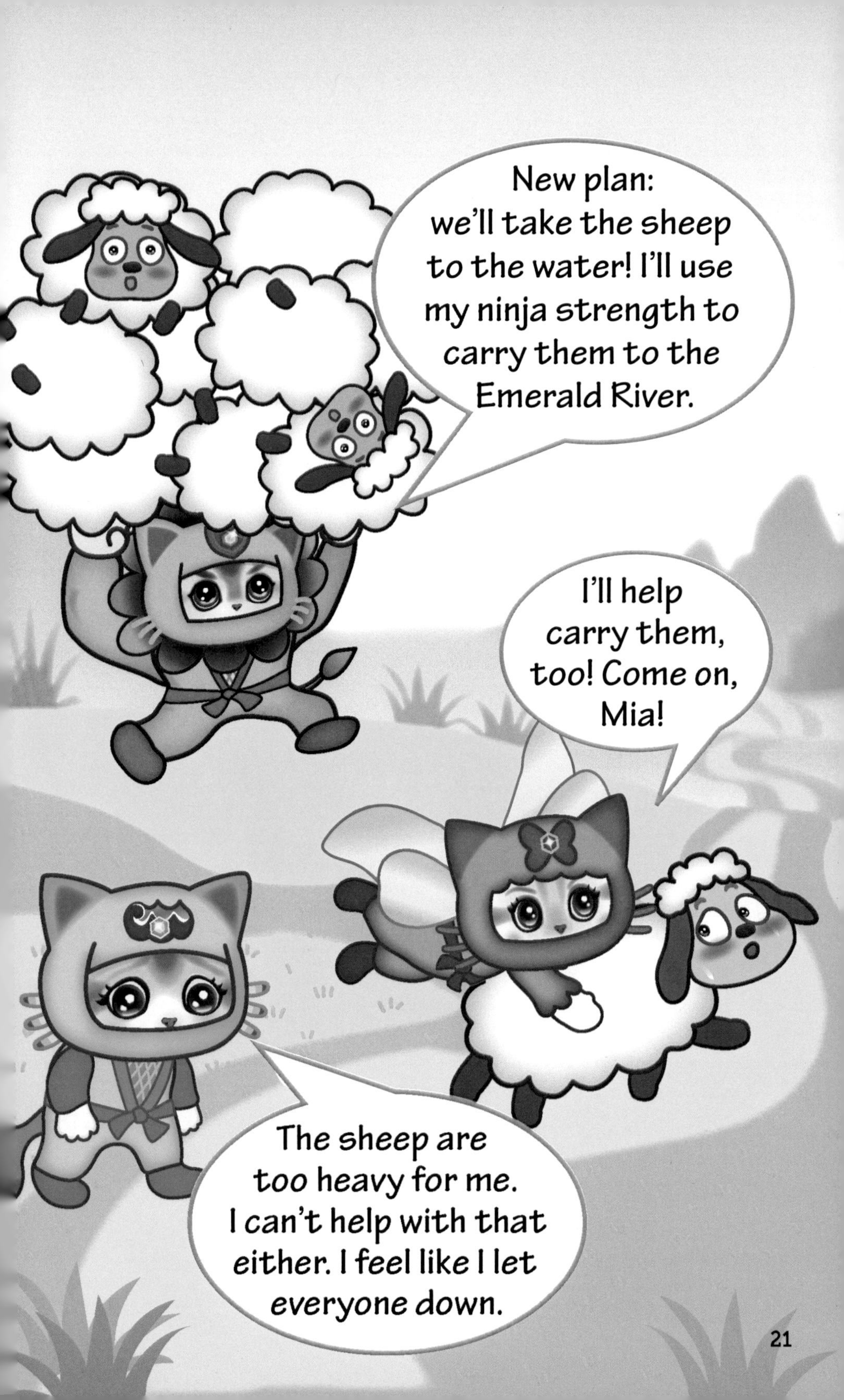
New plan: we'll take the sheep to the water! I'll use my ninja strength to carry them to the Emerald River.
I'll help carry them, too! Come on, Mia!
The sheep are too heavy for me. I can't help with that either. I feel like I let everyone down.

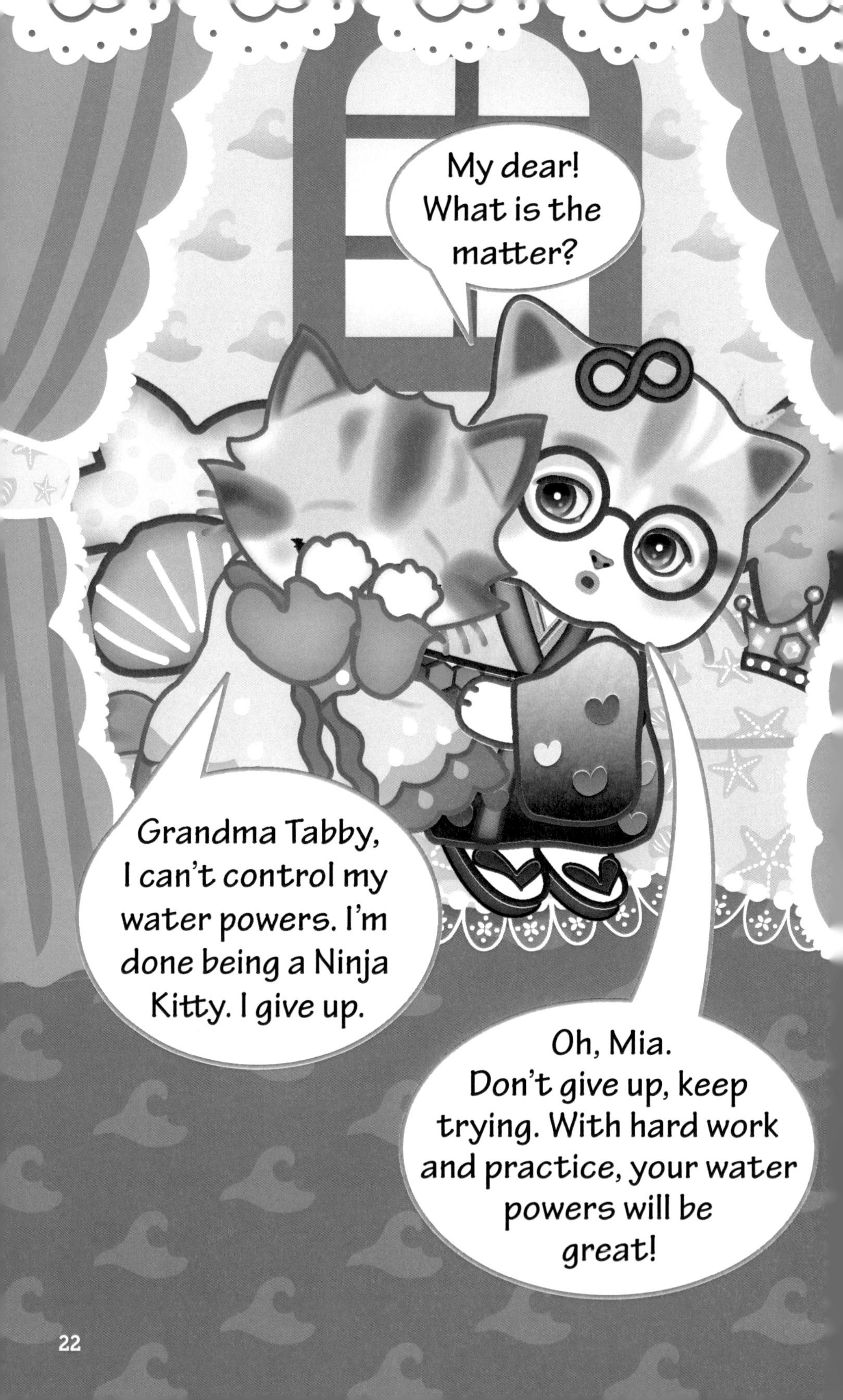
My dear! What is the matter?
Grandma Tabby, I can't control my water powers. I'm done being a Ninja Kitty. I give up.
Oh, Mia. Don't give up, keep trying. With hard work and practice, your water powers will be great!

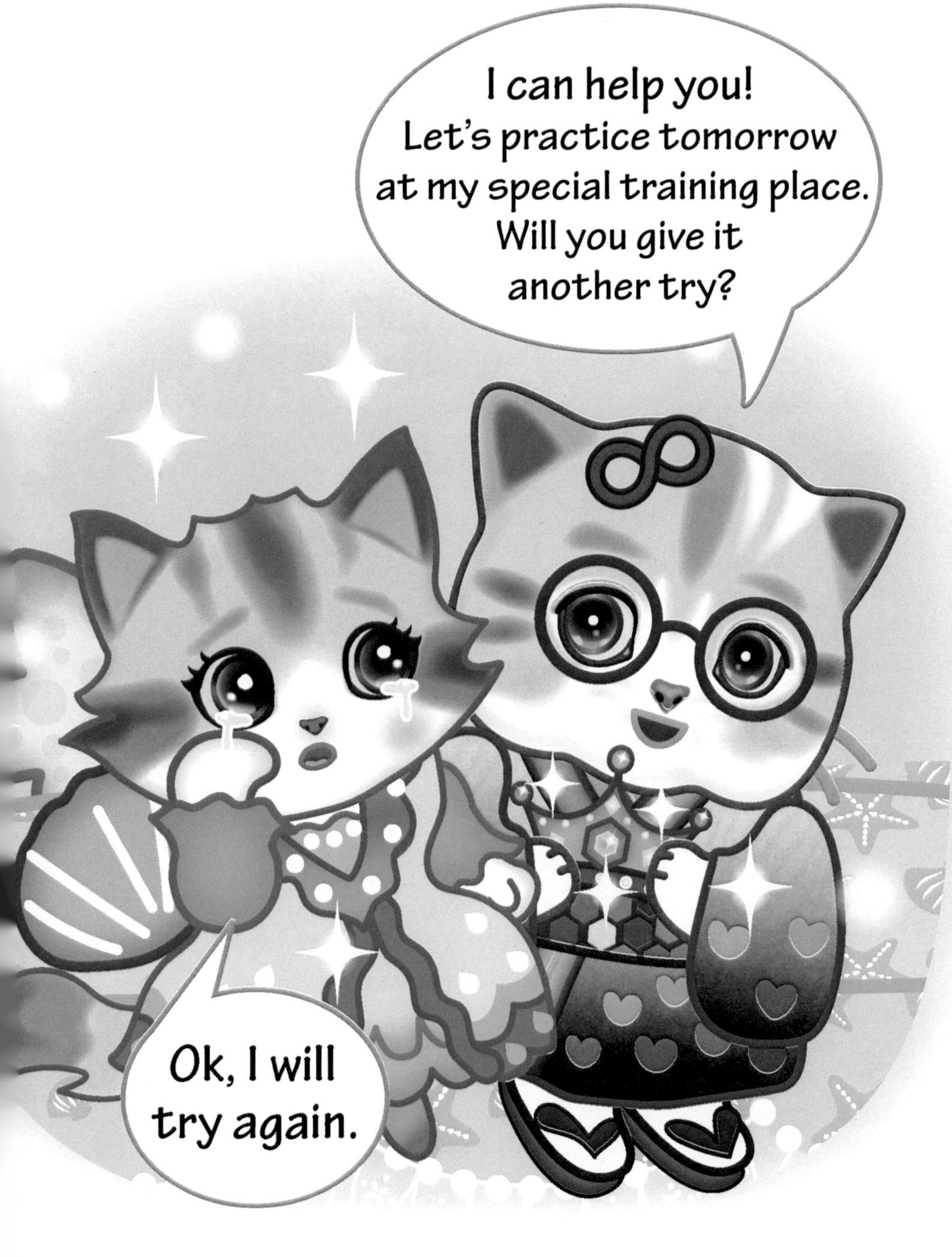
I can help you! Let's practice tomorrow at my special training place. Will you give it another try?
Ok, I will try again.

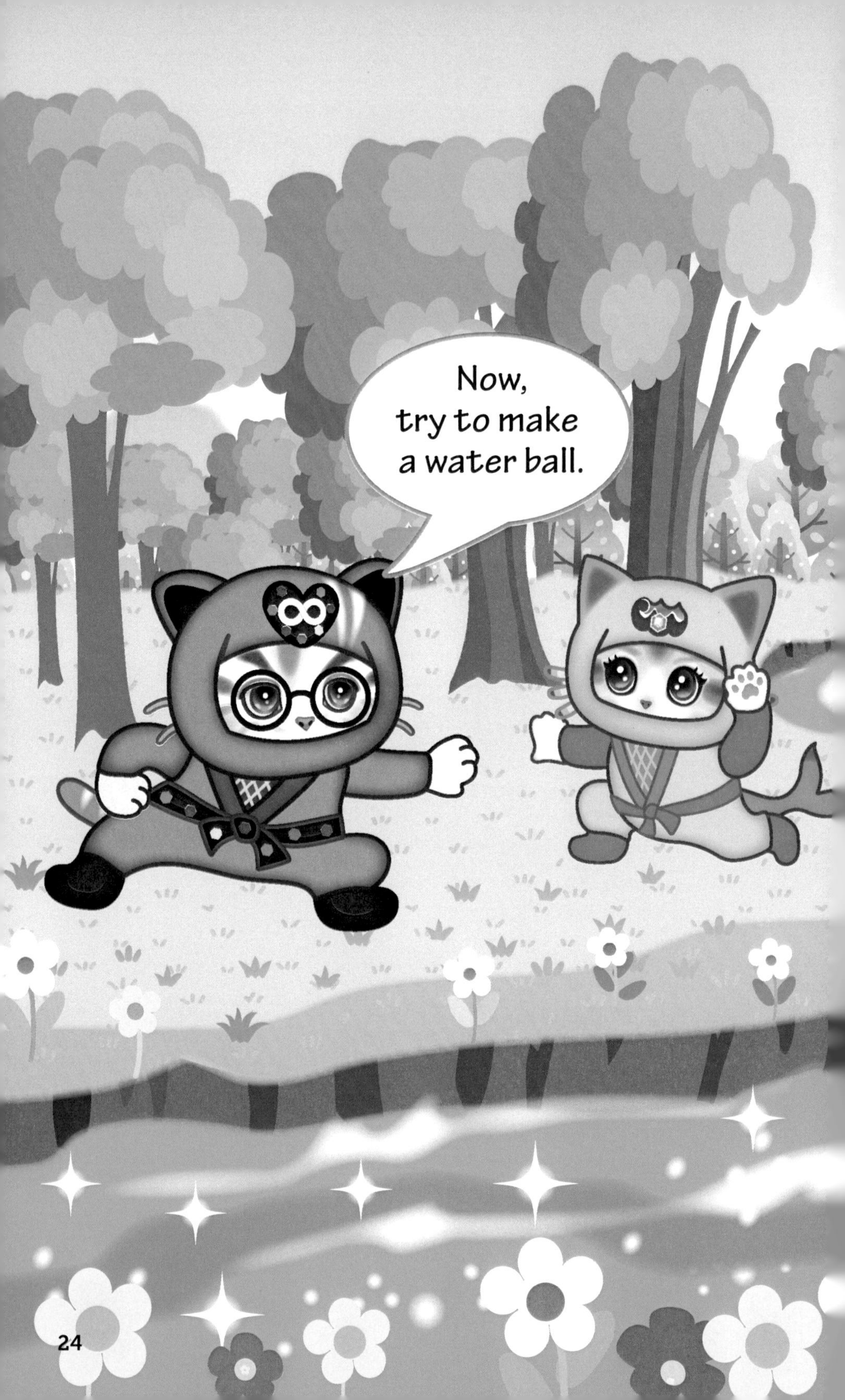
Now, try to make a water ball.

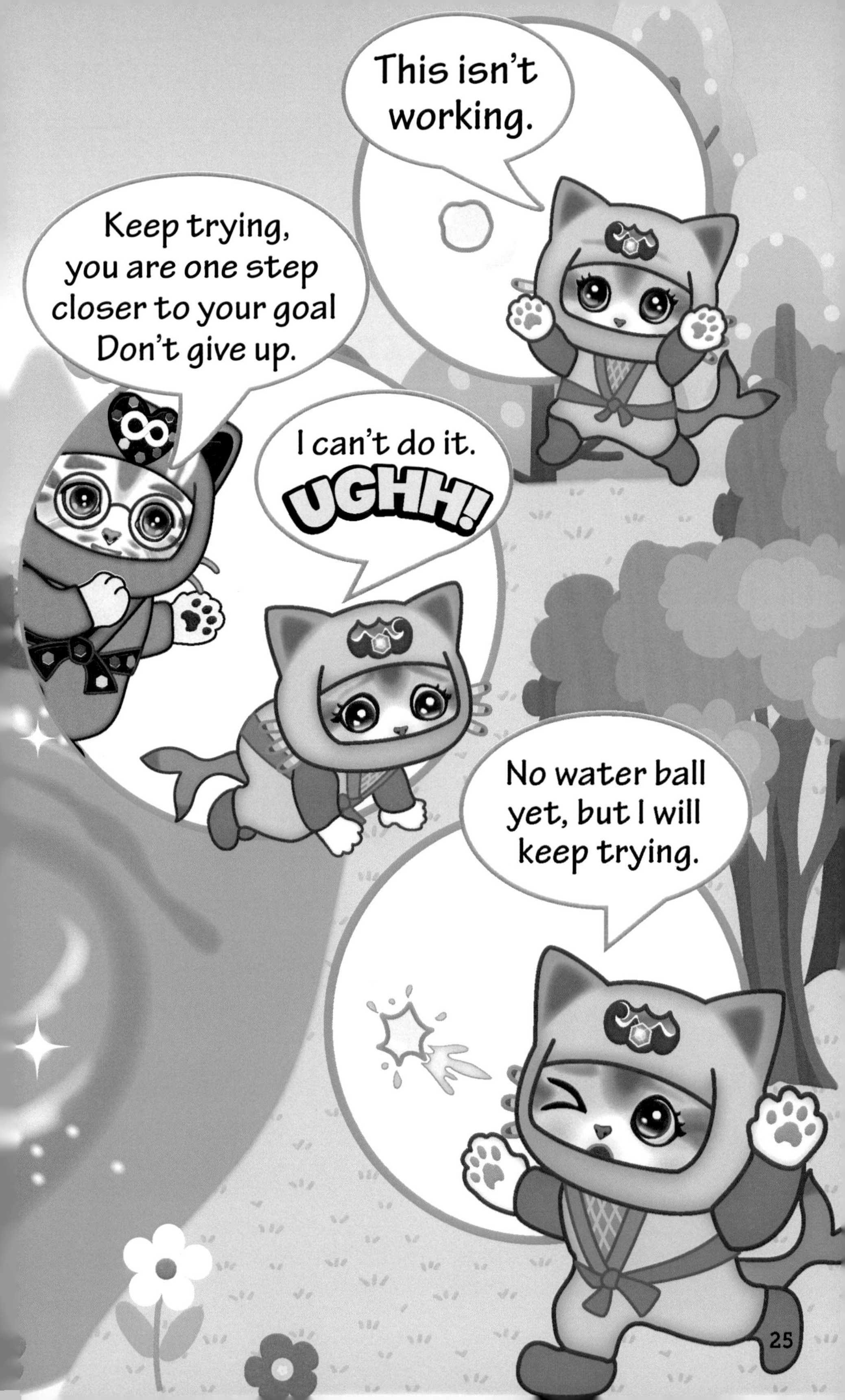
This isn't working.
Keep trying, you are one step closer to your goal Don't give up.
I can't do it.
UGHH!
No water ball yet, but I will keep trying.

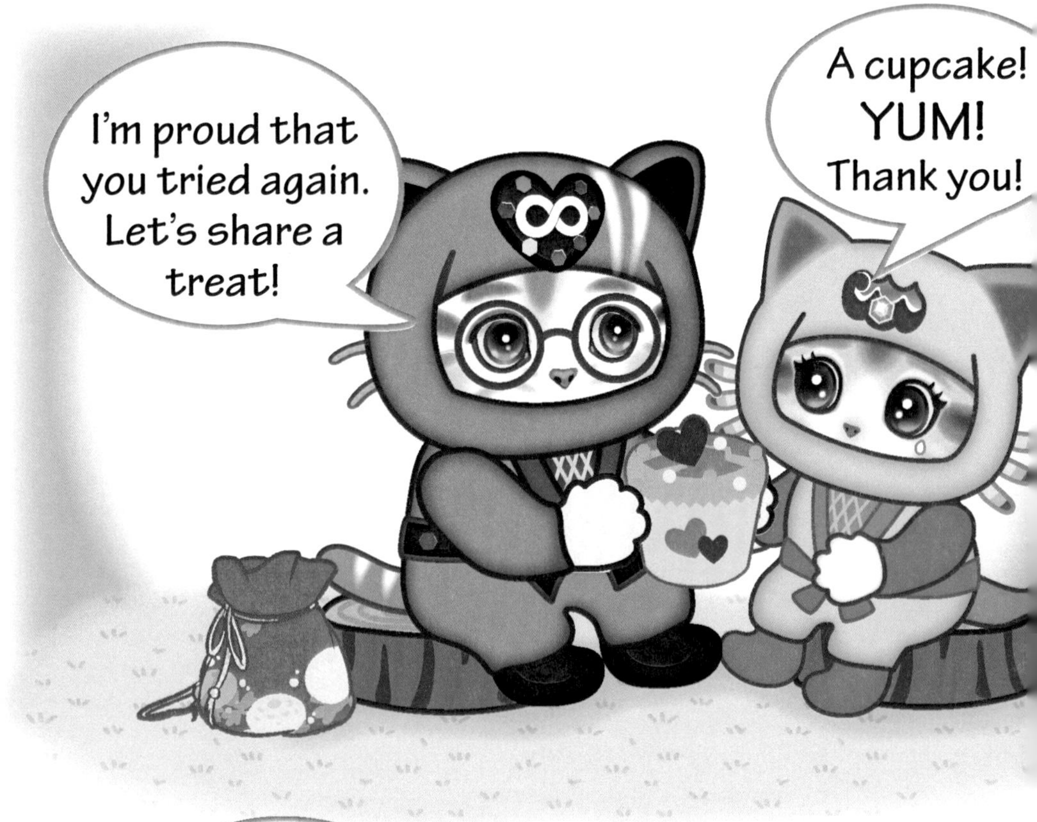
I'm proud that you tried again. Let's share a treat!
A cupcake! YUM! Thank you!

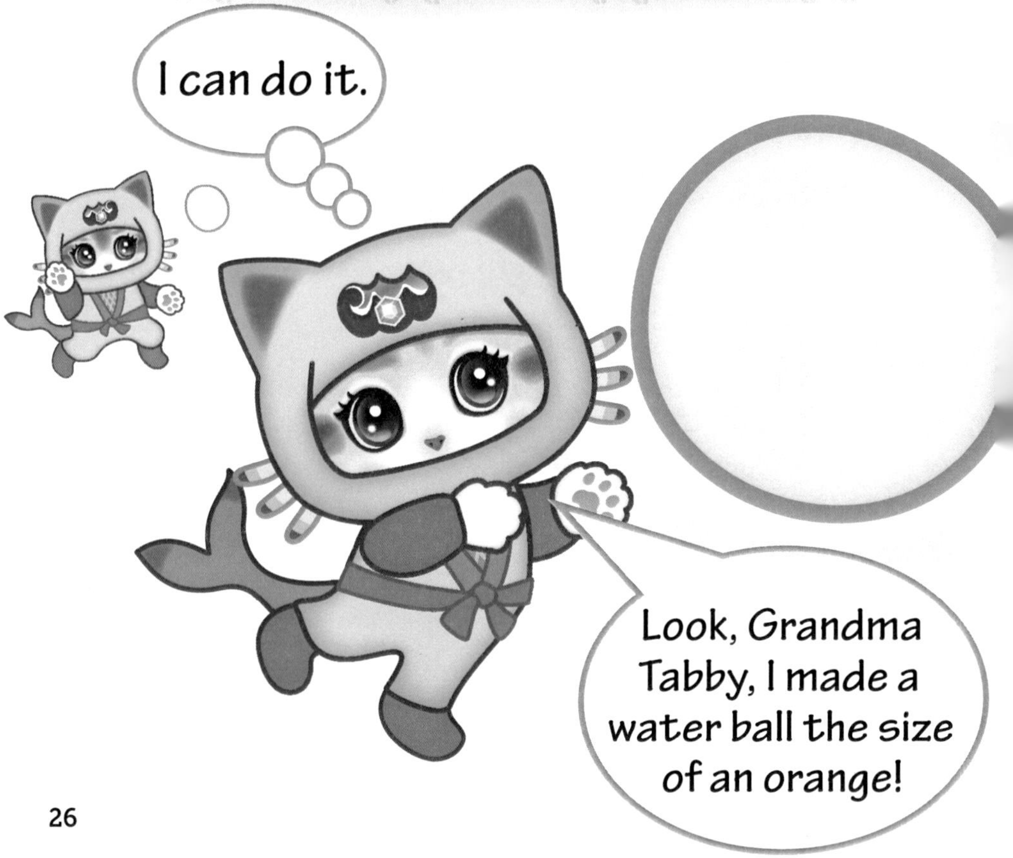
I can do it.
Look, Grandma Tabby, I made a water ball the size of an orange!

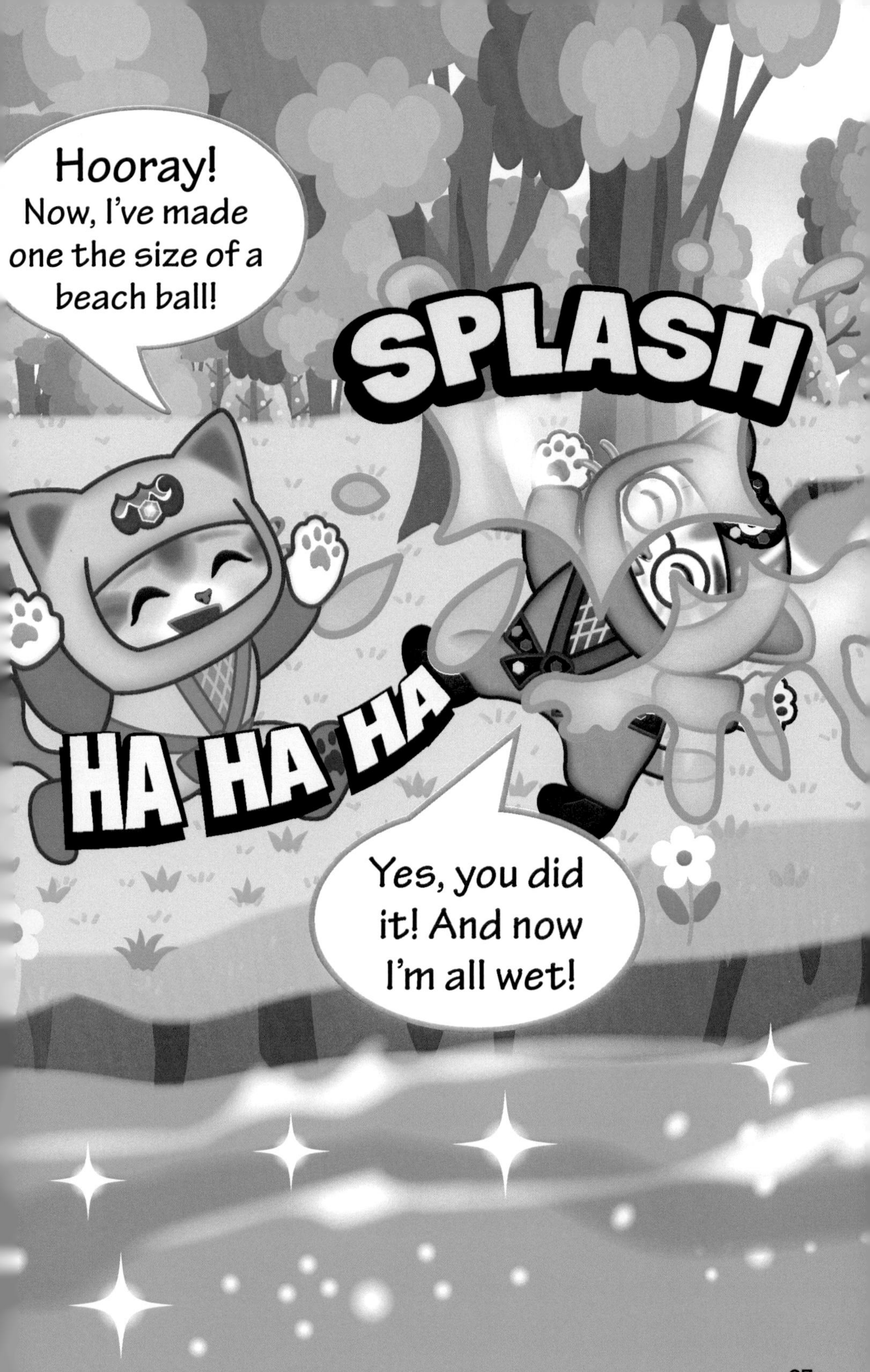
Hooray! Now, I've made one the size of a beach ball!
SPLASH
HA HA HA
Yes, you did it! And now I'm all wet!

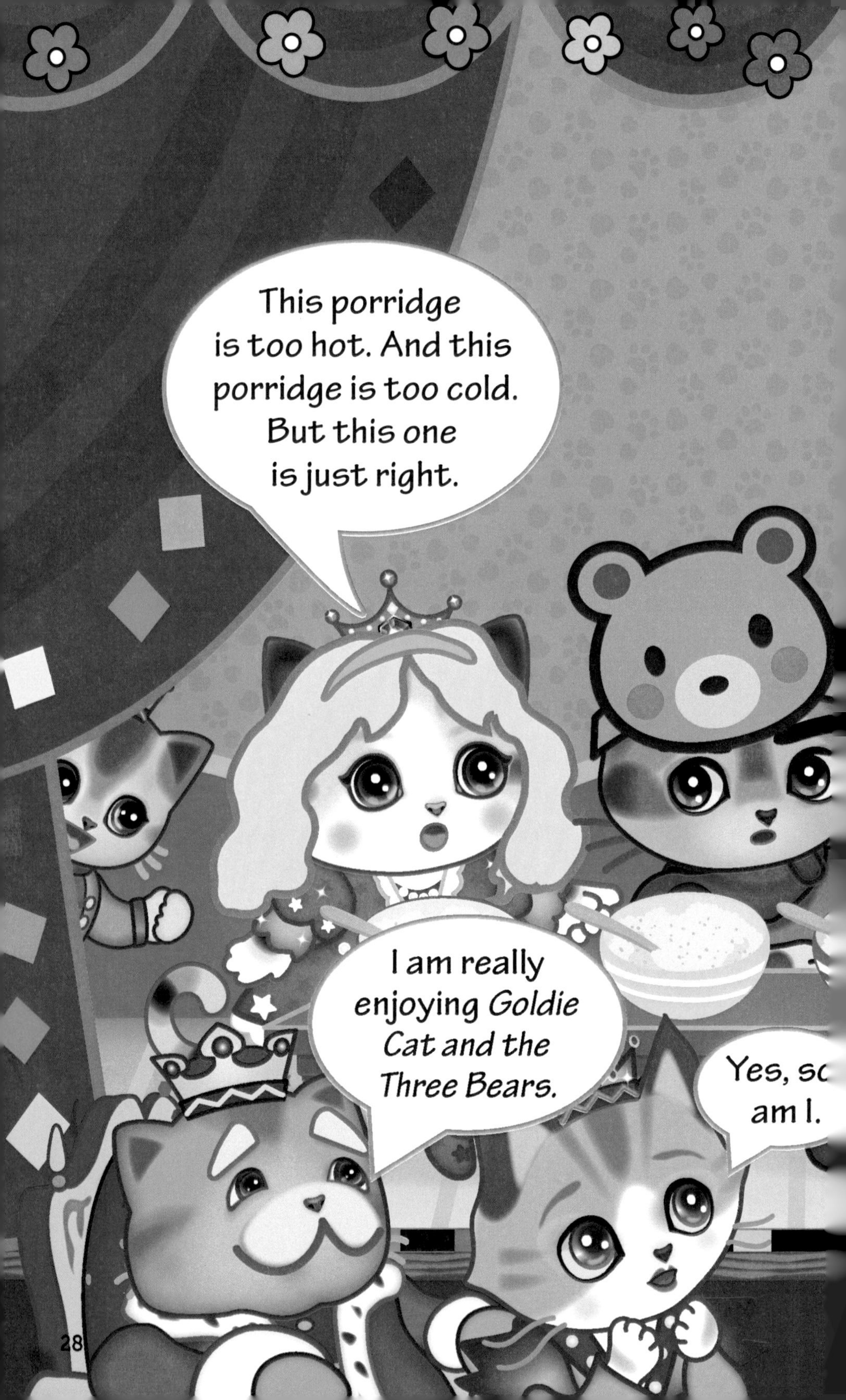
This porridge is too hot. And this porridge is too cold. But this *one* is just right.
I am really enjoying *Goldie Cat and the Three Bears.*
Yes, s am I.

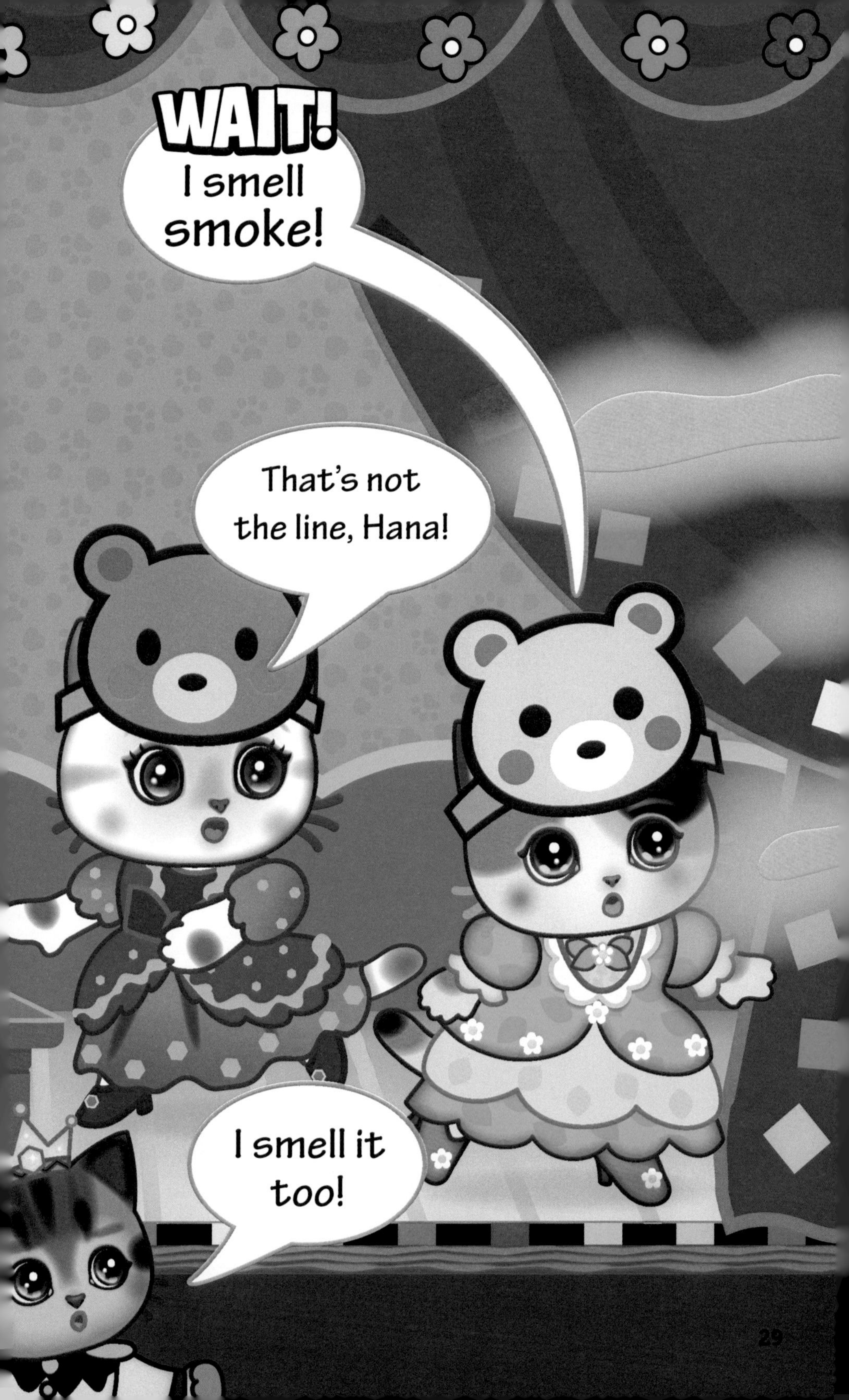
WAIT! I smell smoke!
That's not the line, Hana!
I smell it too!

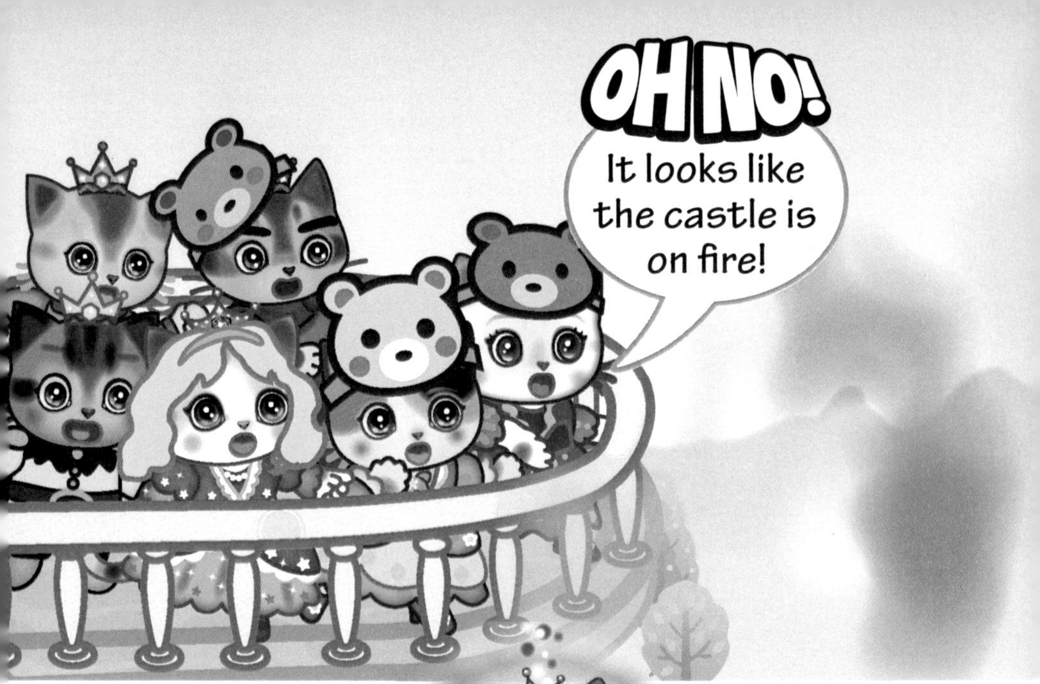
OH NO!
It looks like the castle is on fire!

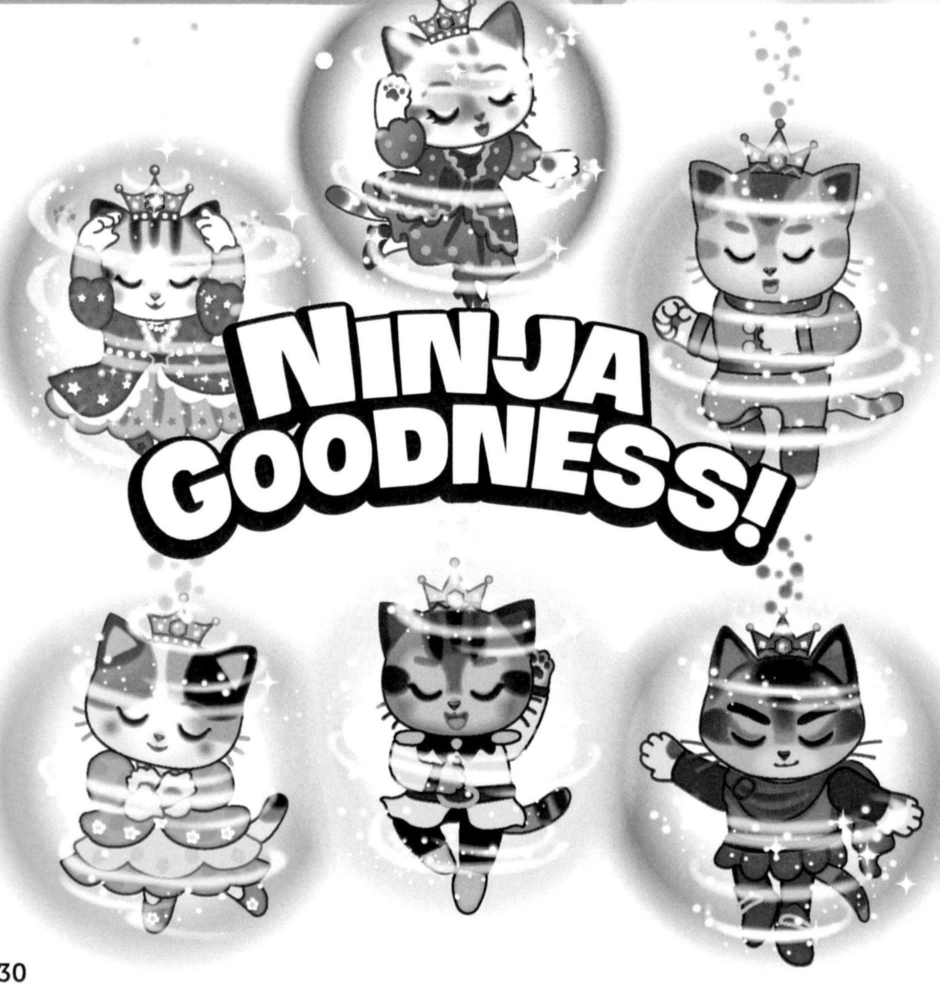
NINJA GOODNESS!

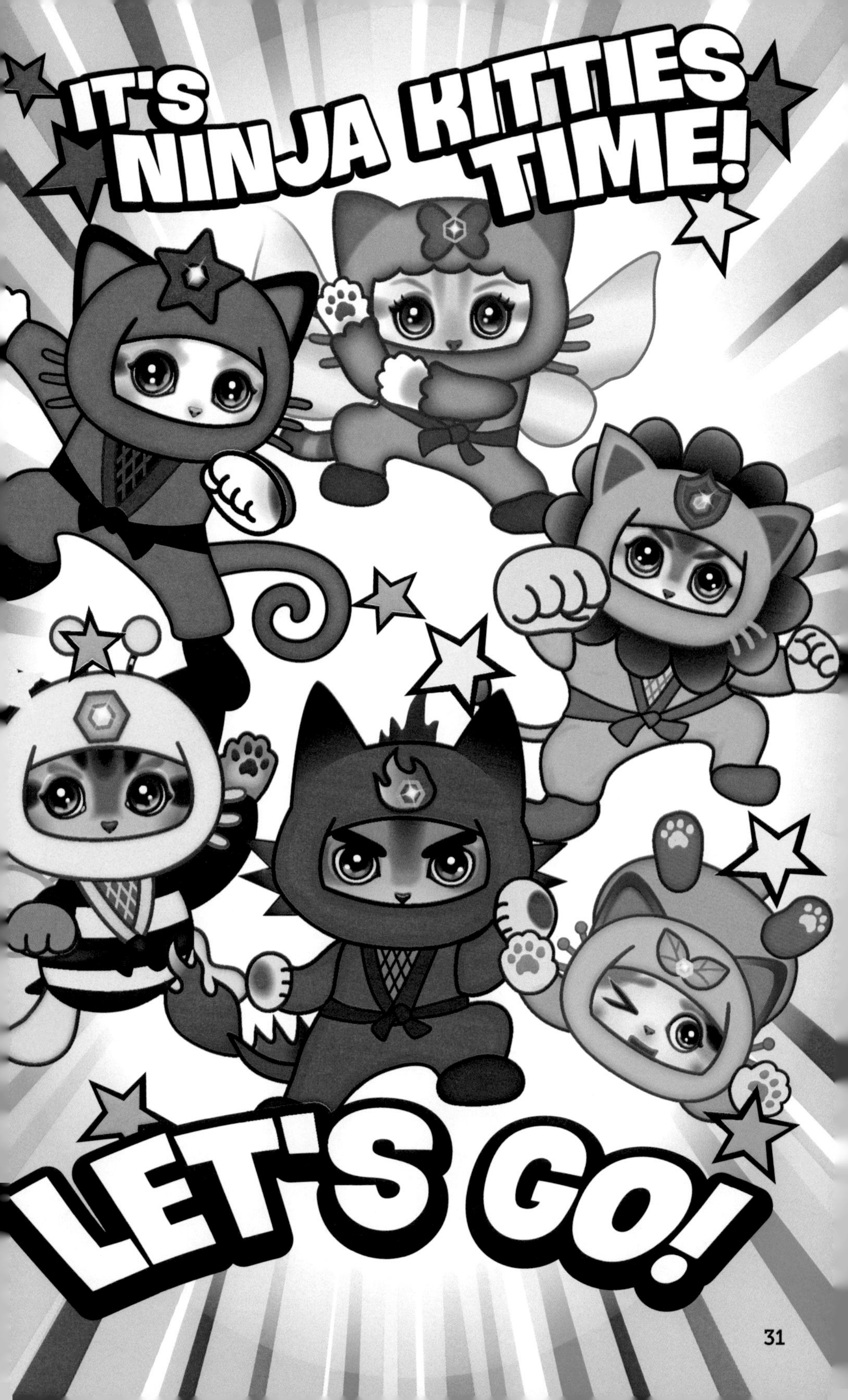
IT'S NINJA KITTIES TIME!
LET'S GO!

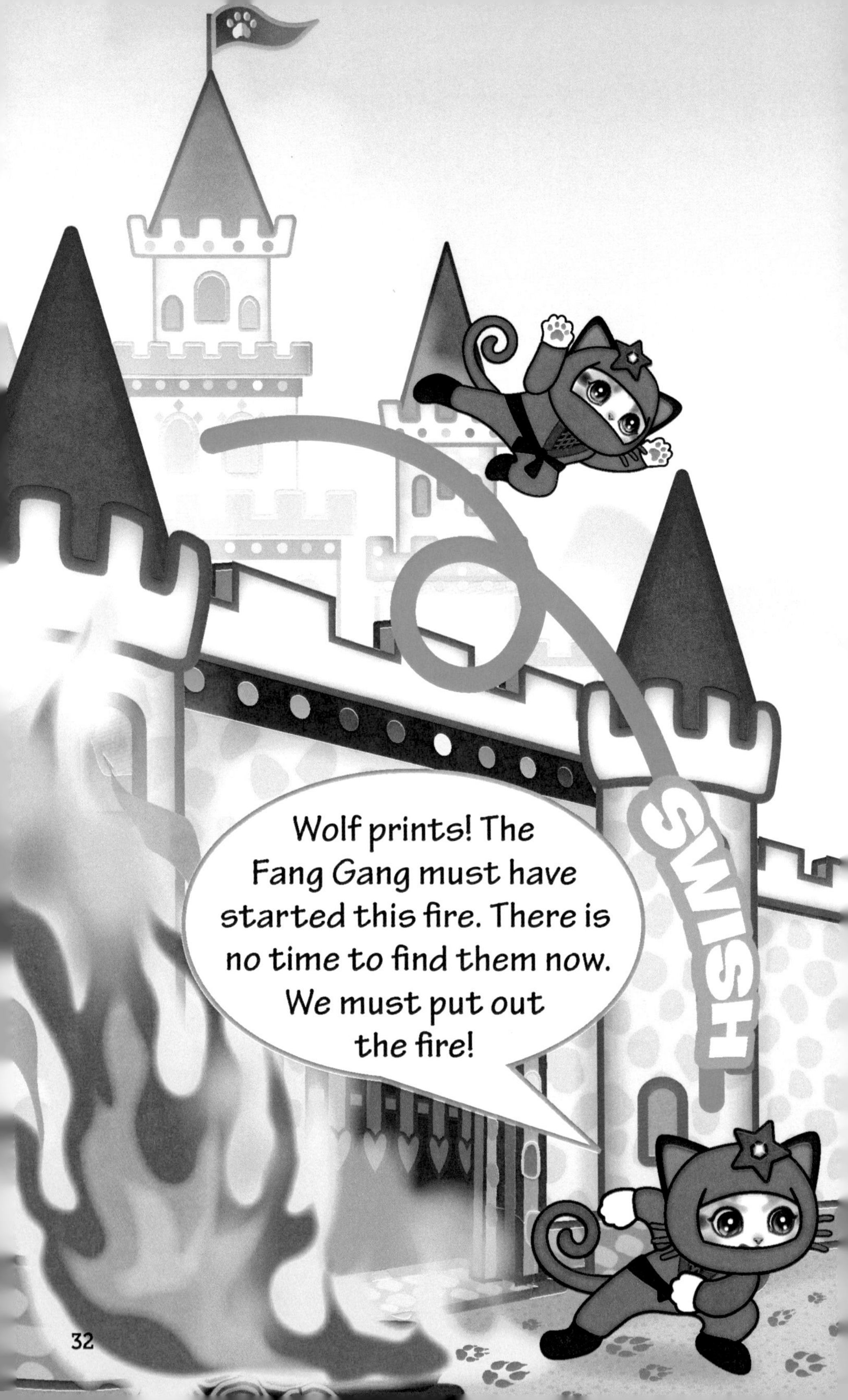
SWISH
Wolf prints! The Fang Gang must have started this fire. There is no time to find them now. We must put out the fire!

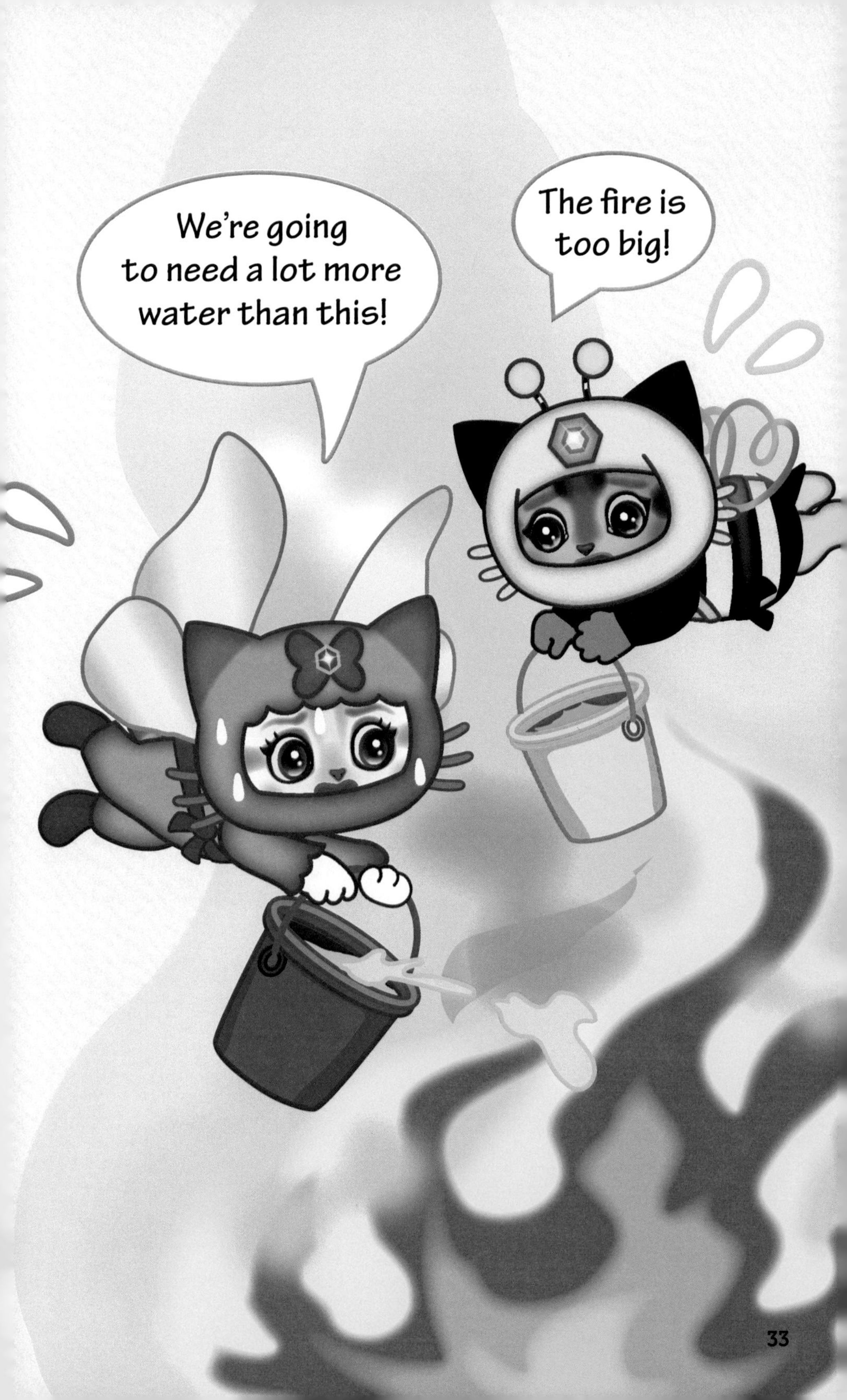
We're going to need a lot more water than this!
The fire is too big!

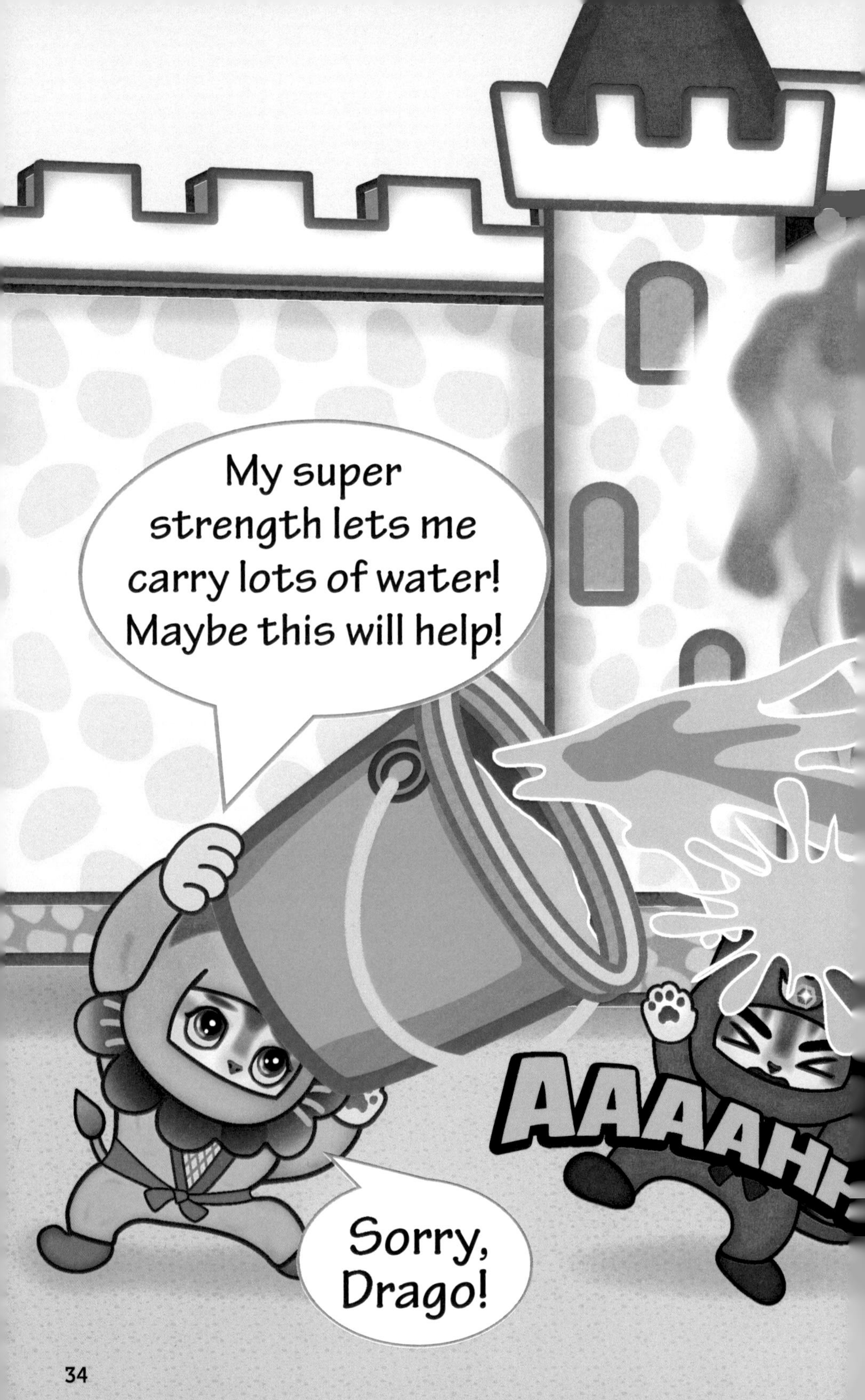
My super strength lets me carry lots of water! Maybe this will help!
AAAAAHH
Sorry, Drago!

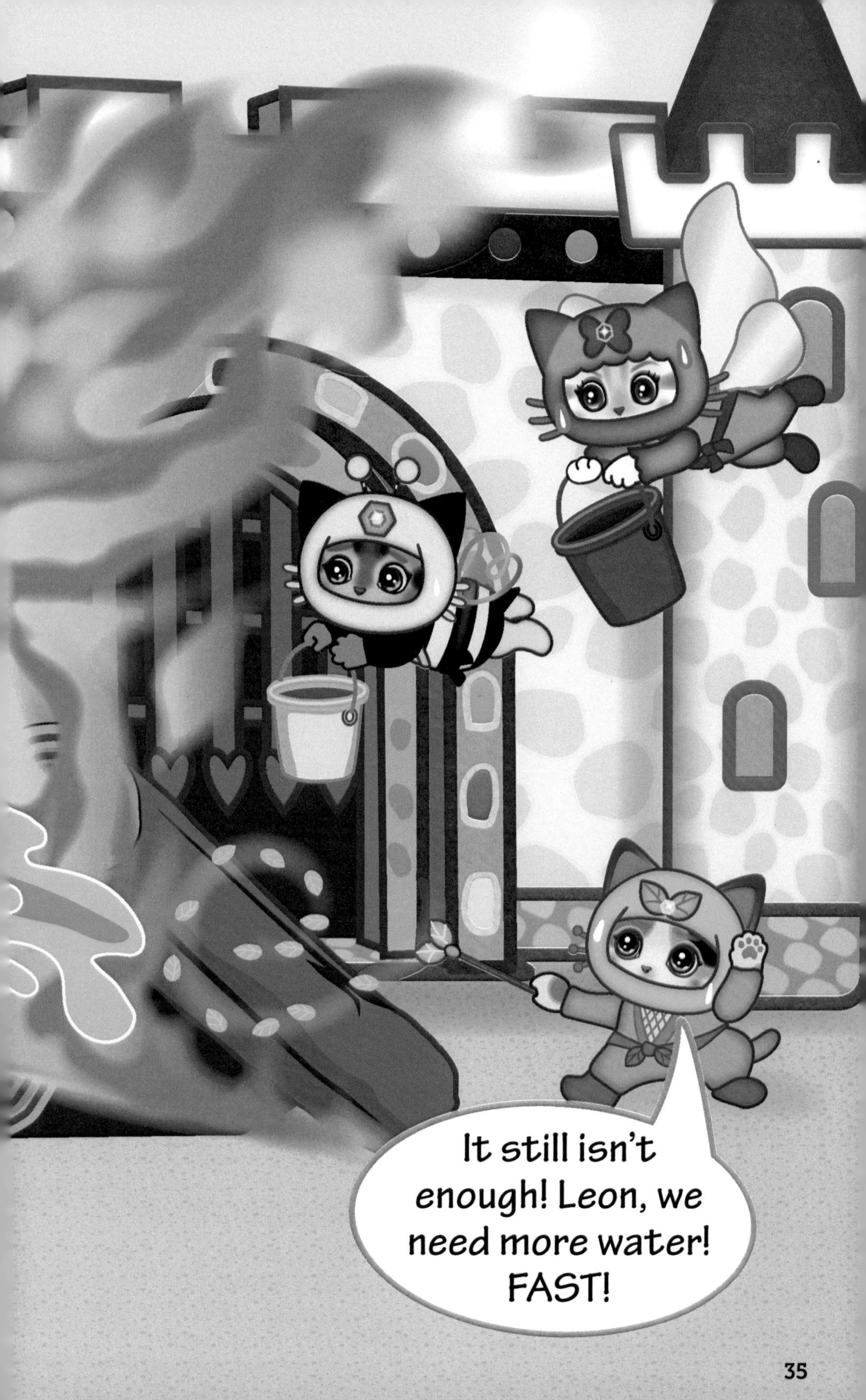
It still isn't enough! Leon, we need more water! FAST!

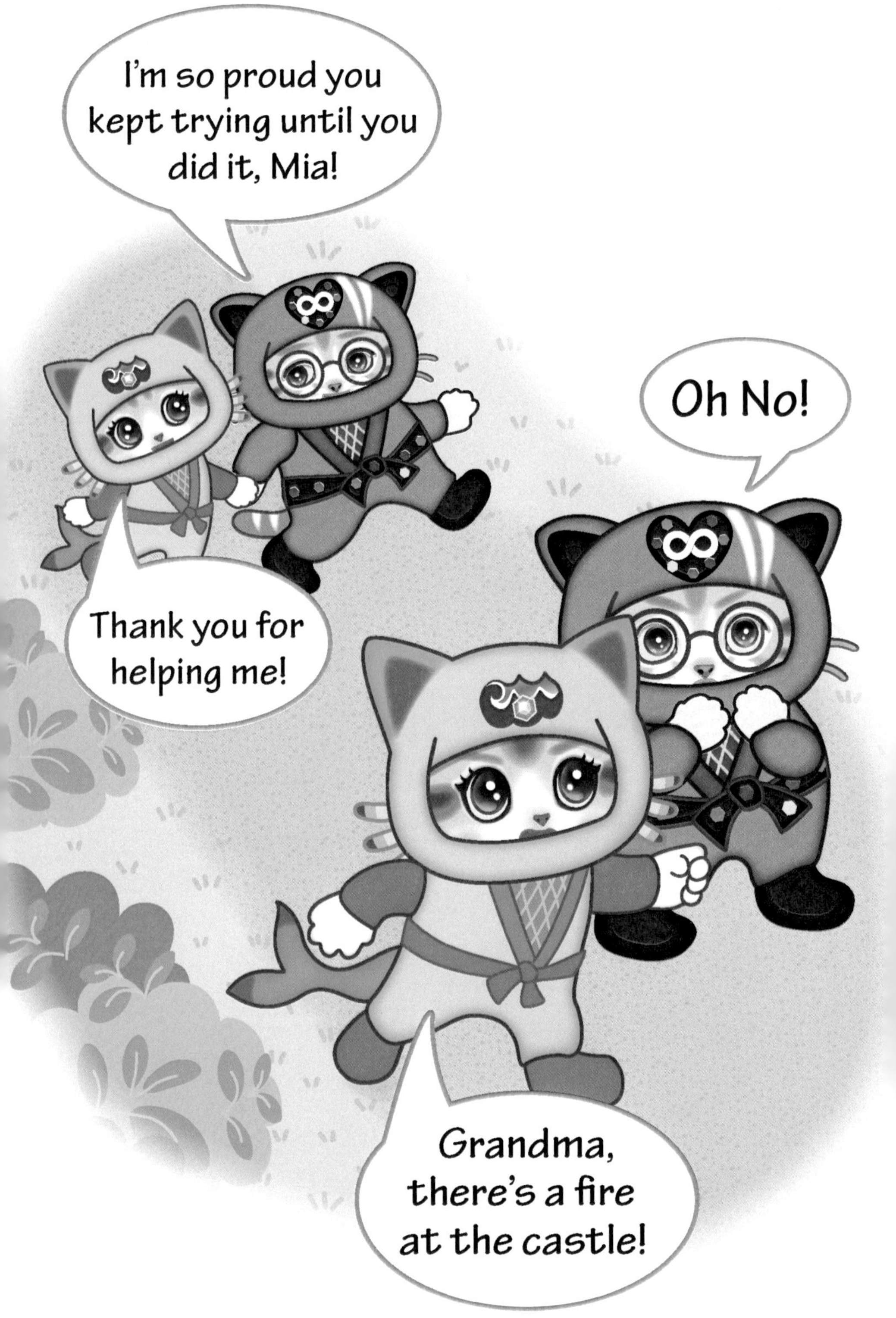
I'm so proud you kept trying until you did it, Mia!
Thank you for helping me!
Oh No!
Grandma, there's a fire at the castle!

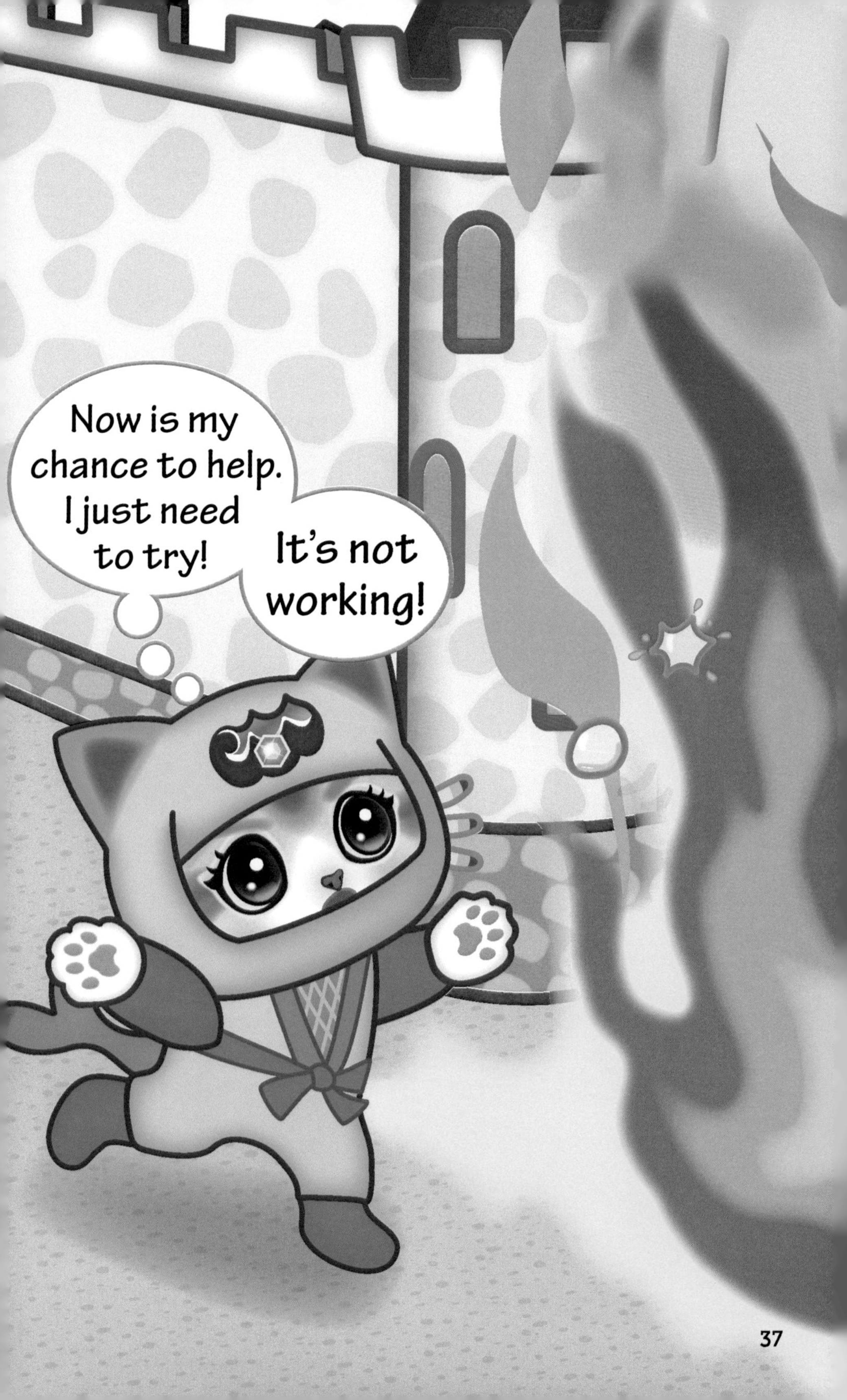
Now is my chance to help. I just need to try!
It's not working!

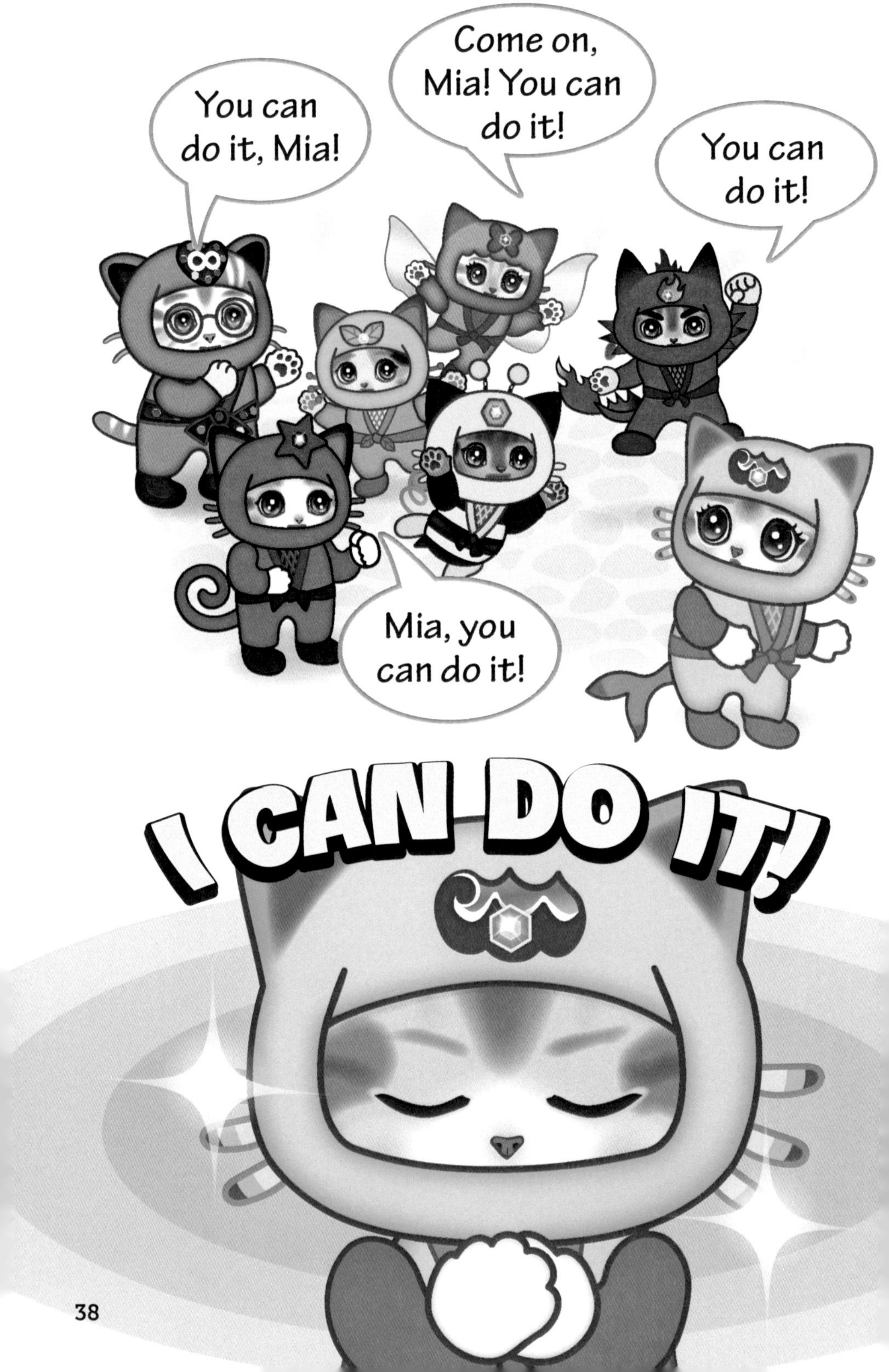
You can do it, Mia!
Come on, Mia! You can do it!
You can do it!
Mia, you can do it!
I CAN DO IT!

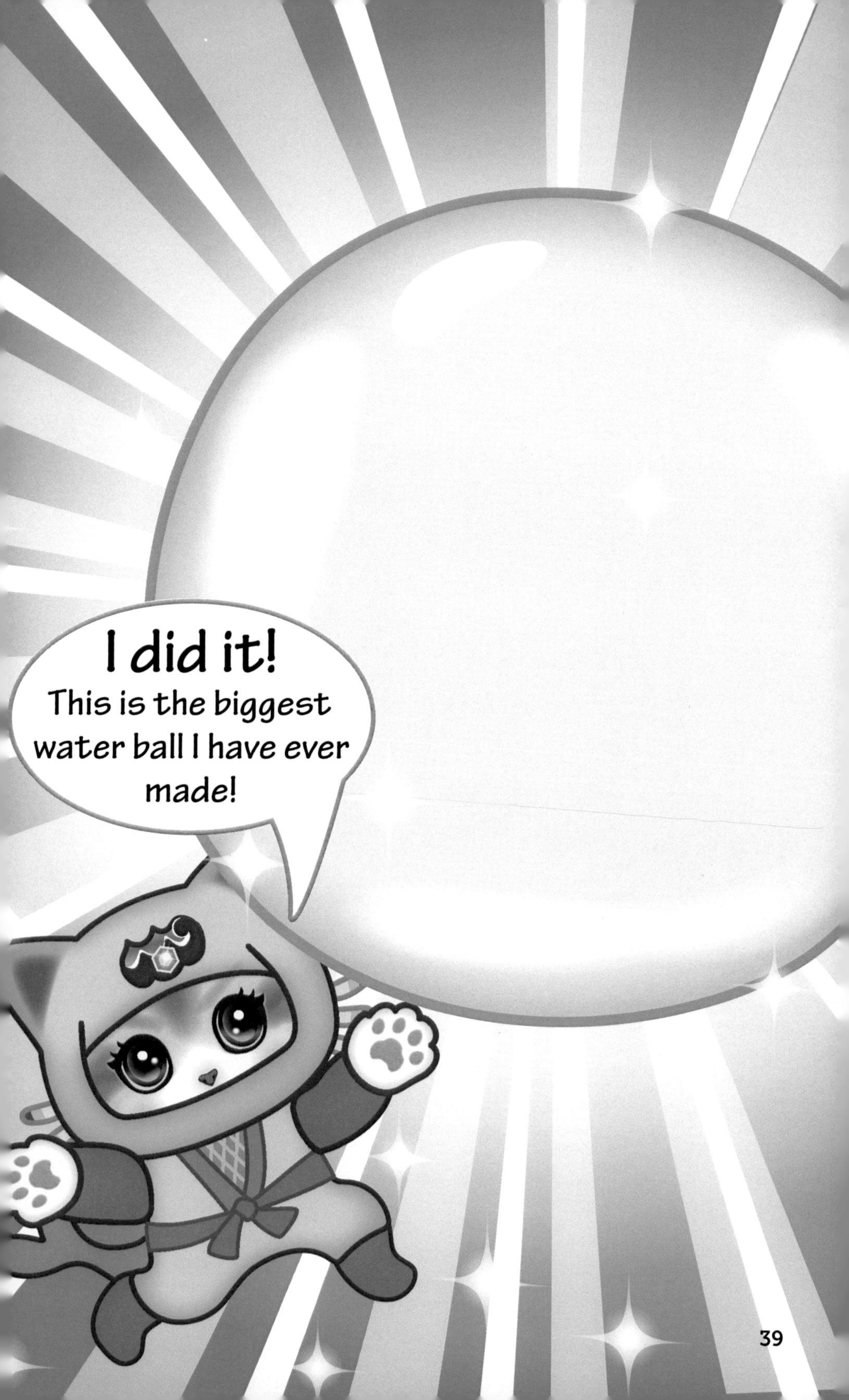
I did it! This is the biggest water ball I have ever made!

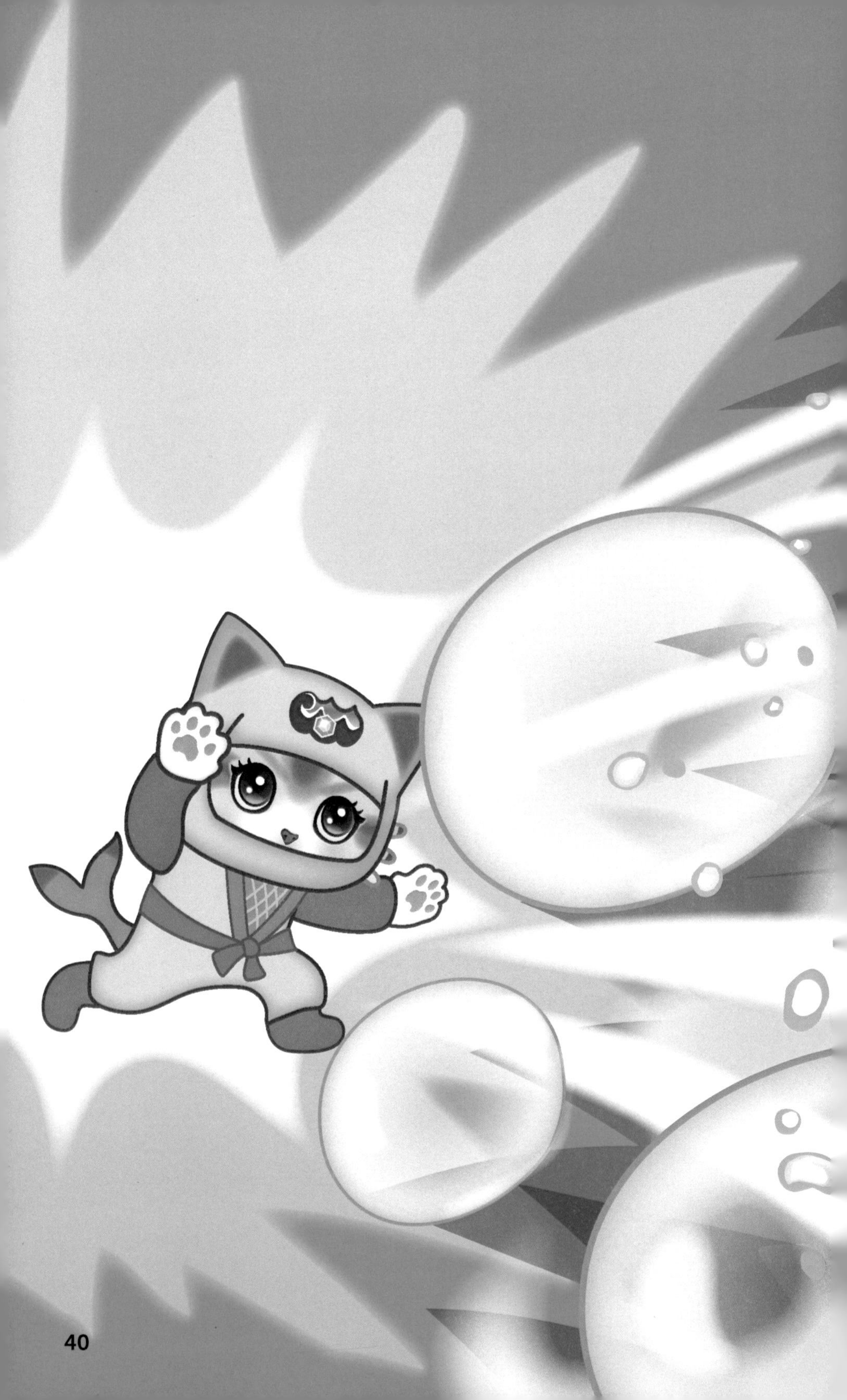

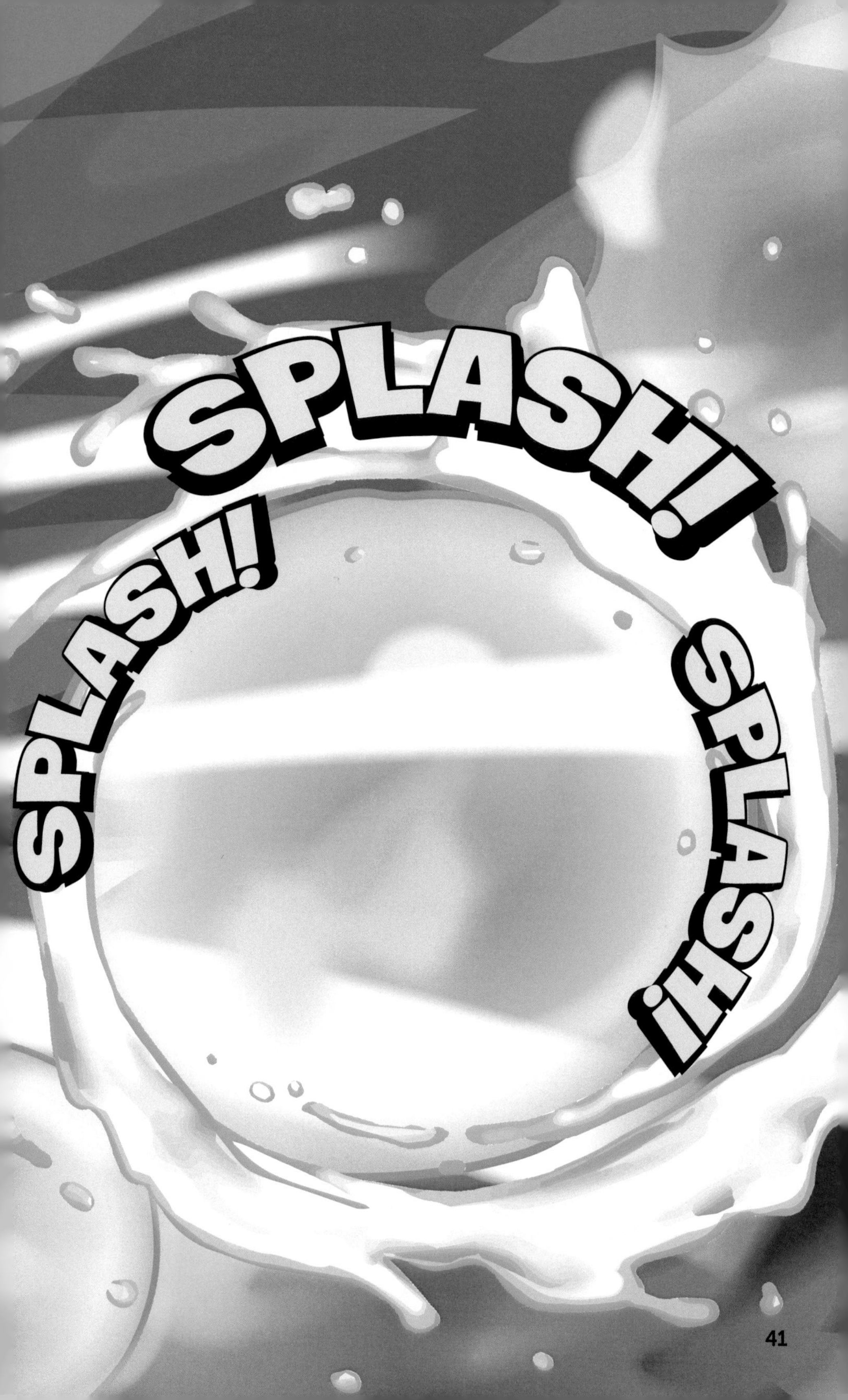
SPLASH!
SPLASH!
SPLASH!

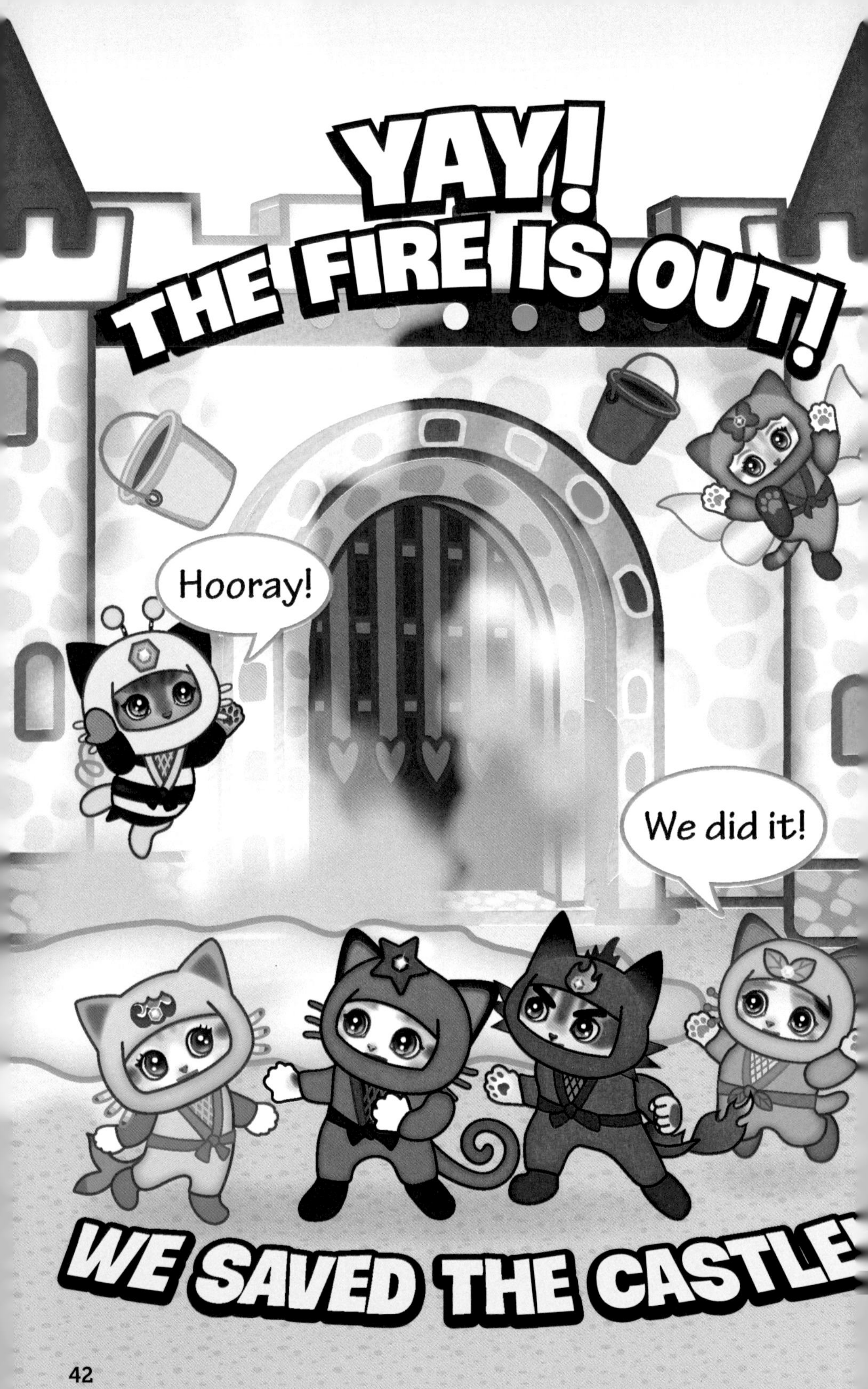
YAY!
THE FIRE IS OUT!
Hooray!
We did it!
WE SAVED THE CASTLE!

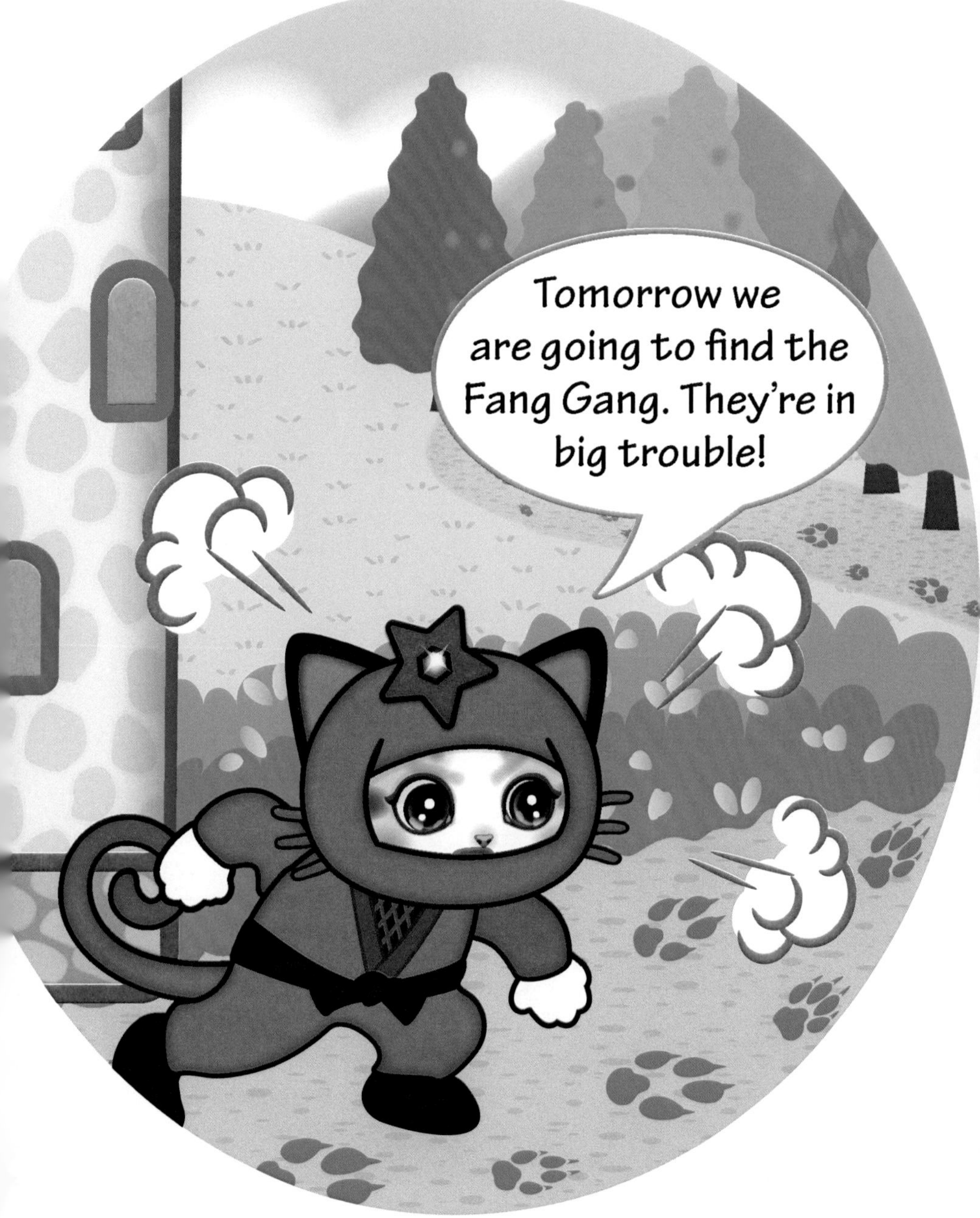
Tomorrow we are going to find the Fang Gang. They're in big trouble!

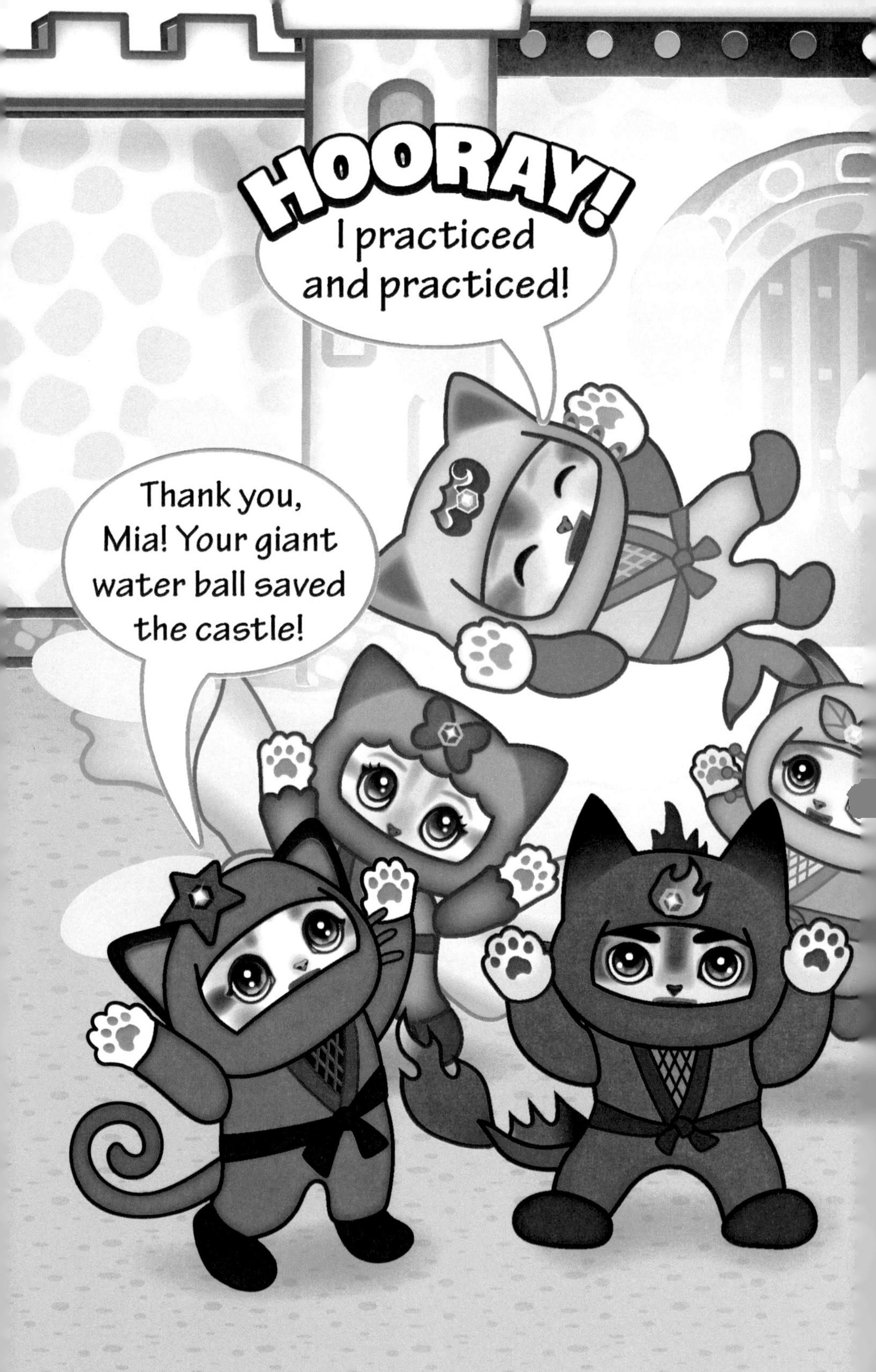
HOORAY!
I practiced and practiced!
Thank you, Mia! Your giant water ball saved the castle!

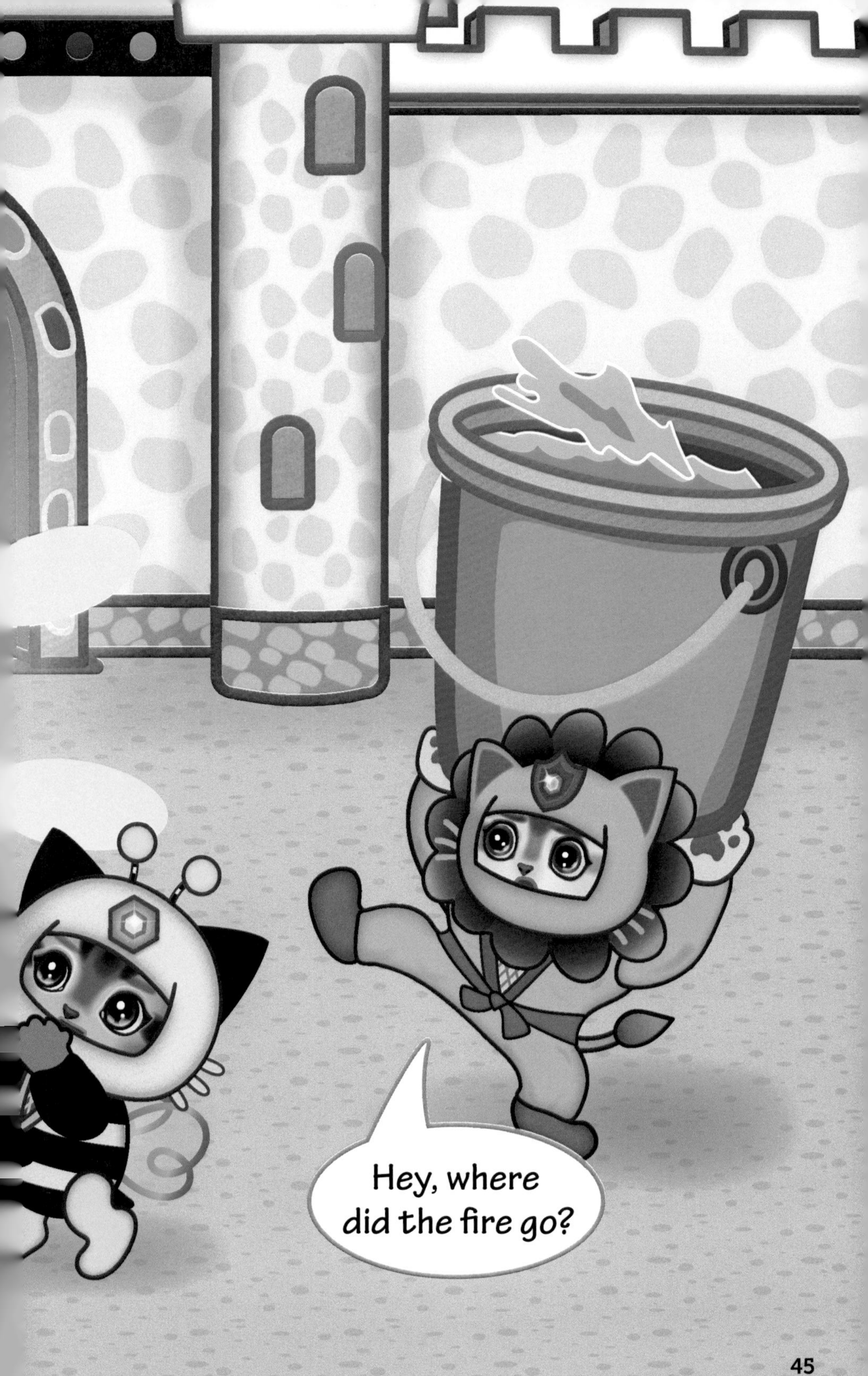
Hey, where did the fire go?

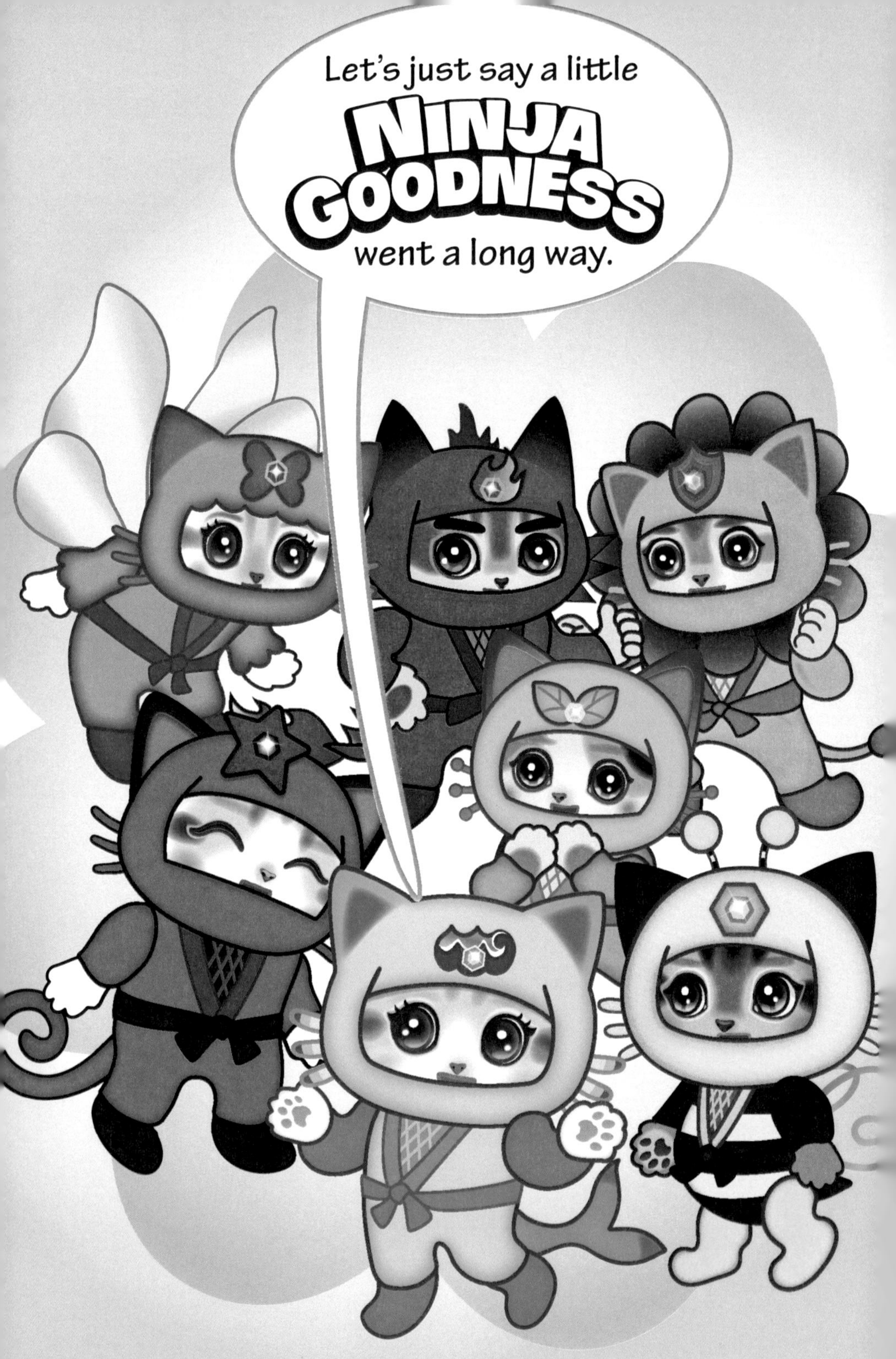
Let's just say a little
NINJA GOODNESS
went a long way.

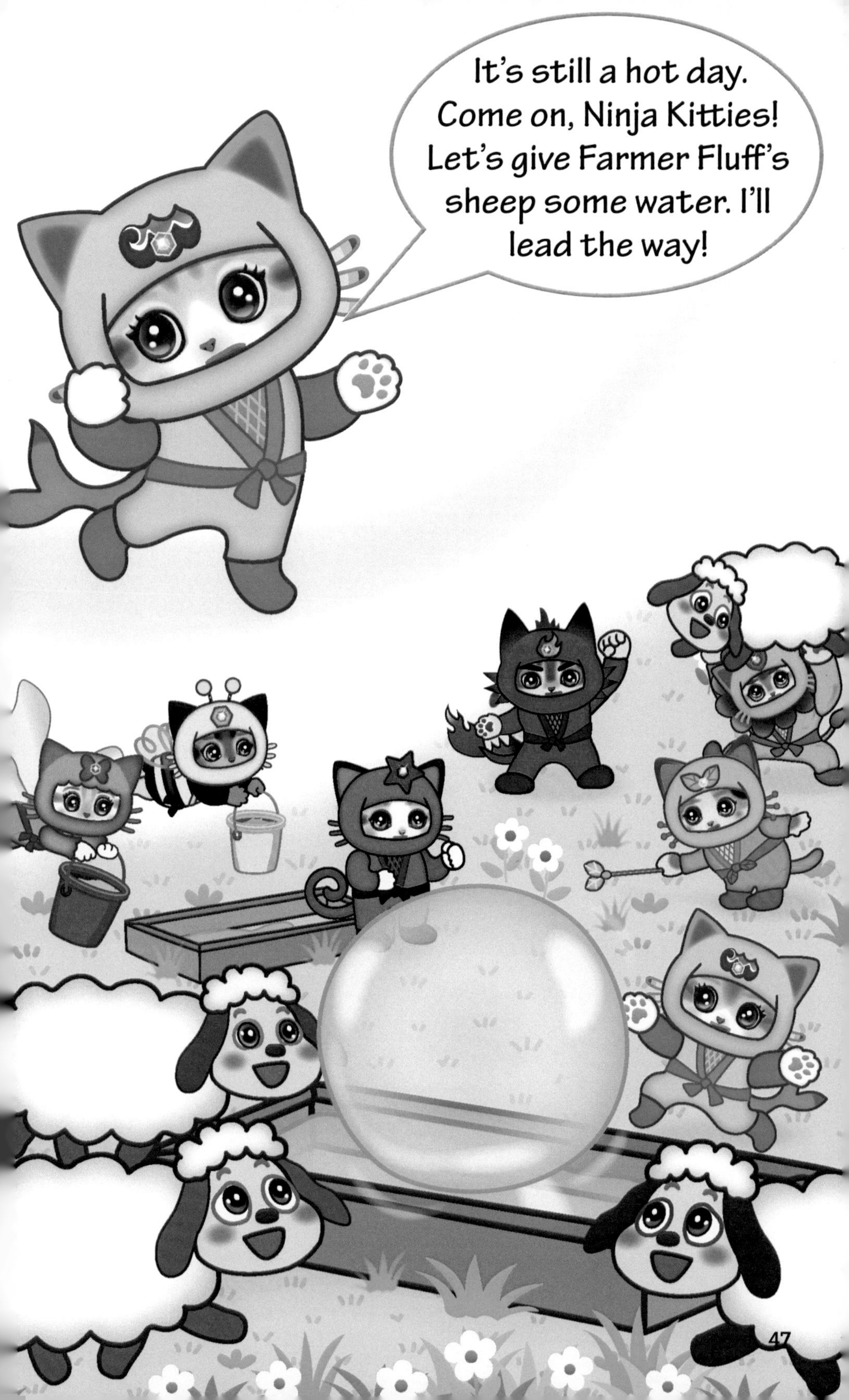
It's still a hot day. Come on, Ninja Kitties! Let's give Farmer Fluff's sheep some water. I'll lead the way!

Grandma Tabby's Ninja Lesson

Sometimes it's hard to master your skills or learn new things. But Mia showed us that if you keep trying and don't give up, you will succeed!

NINJA GOODNESS!

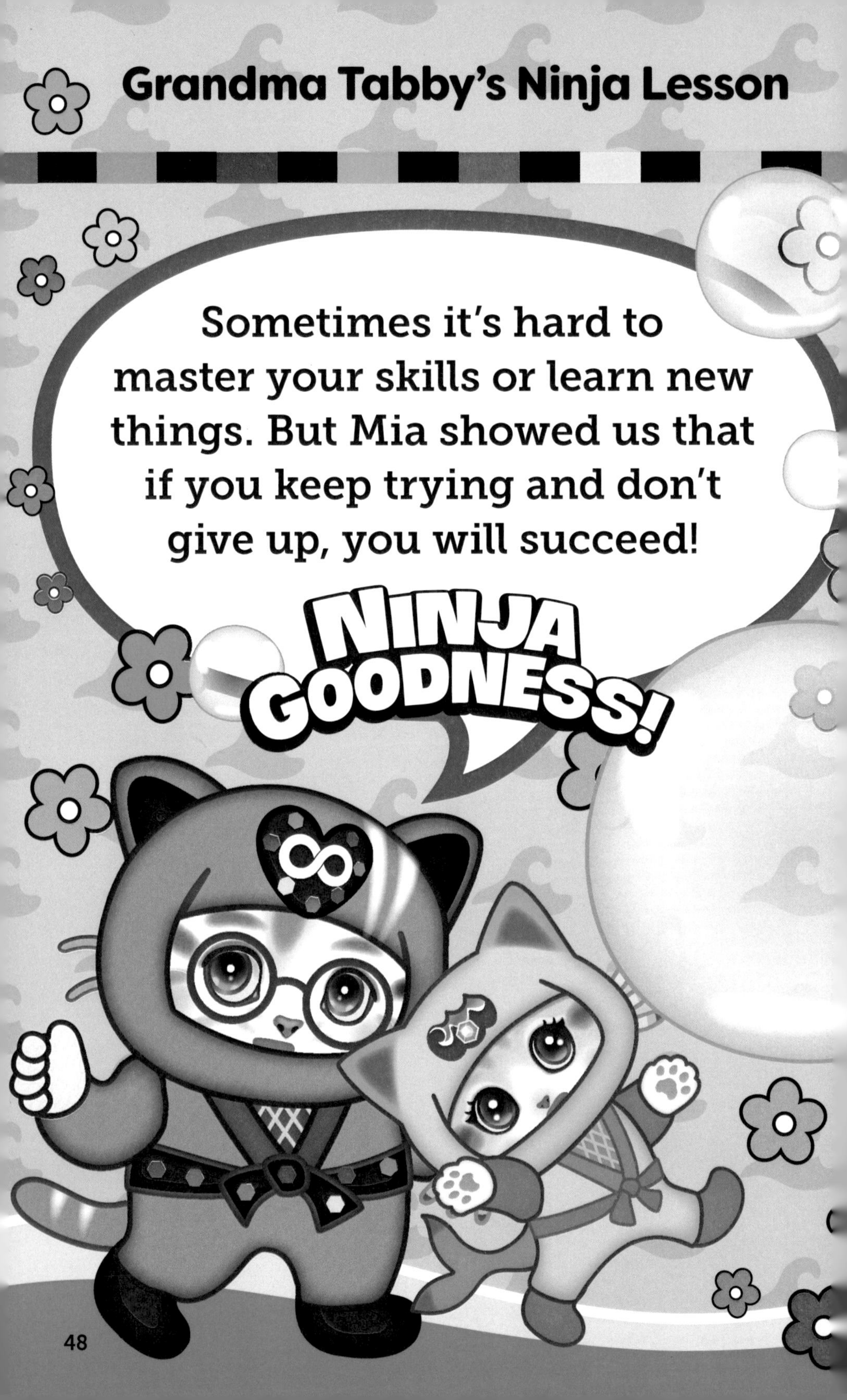